Transport

———————

Joan Zahm

———————

To

Gary, Jen and Linda

For a million reasons, all of which circle back to

love

For small creatures such as we,
the vastness is bearable only through love.
Carl Sagan, American Astronomer

1

The awakening was unexpected.

Perhaps the abrupt and total silence alerted the slumbering brain. The mind fought it, wanting to keep traveling over the water with wind in the hair, and flowing as only dreams can do, through clouds and rooms and places she knew, but had bizarrely changed. Thirst and an abnormal metallic taste combined forces to fight the dreams until the eyes opened.

She lay there for some time, looking at her surroundings with a blank mind, strangely calm. At some point she sat up, feeling light headed, only allowing her eyes to roam the room. When her head cleared, she turned and saw that the faint light in the bare room was coming from a high window behind her, suggesting late evening or early morning. She stood up slowly, keeping a hand on the bed for steadiness. *Such a small, plain room.* Her body stood motionless, but her eyes raced around the unadorned walls, whipped back and skidded to a stop on the bed. A step back gave a full view of the bed with its wide central support, digital monitors, a dark screen and, on each end, a plate of unique transparent material extending toward the floor. She studied it for several moments, but her stares produced no insight.

No water. She approached what looked like a door opposite the window, but finding no handle, began pushing the panel and surrounding area. No response. She sat back on the bed, her heart pounding from the small exertion, and surveyed the room again. She noticed a column of drawers almost seamlessly built into the wall, which somehow reminded her of a ship. Investigating, she found that she could open only one drawer, and it was empty. As she was walking toward the opposite wall, the door released without warning and opened.

She walked out into a hallway. *Ah, a hotel, but no carpet, maybe a ship.* The ceiling was not overly high and had sturdy, gray curved support beams spaced evenly apart. Maybe a military ship she guessed, thinking nothing more of it, as if it were a perfectly ordinary occurrence to wake up thirsty on a military ship. Down the hall stood two men, who appeared to be carefully inspecting a small wall monitor beside a closed door. They turned to continue to the next door when they noticed her, immediately approaching with a determined stiff stride. They stopped abruptly and spoke in a language she could not understand.

"I was looking for some water," was all she could think to say.

They regarded her carefully until the near one said, now quite clearly, "Welcome, Mara, we will take you back to the room."

She studied them more closely. They seemed thin and narrow shouldered with slicked back dark hair, plain long-sleeved tan shirts, nondescript pants, and shoes. She became self-consciously aware of her own covering, consisting of only a loosely fitting blue, sleeveless garment that fell to the middle of her thighs.

Her mind failed to produce a reply when all colors began to leave her vision, turning her world into muted, gray tones just as her legs began a slow-motion collapse. Her body started a soundless slide to the floor, saved only by the men's rapid response of grabbing each of her arms and looking as if they were supporting a rubbery puppet. *Very strong for their thin appearance.*

Through the haze, she watched one move his hand and begin speaking in the foreign language. Rapid footsteps soon approached. Two men advanced around the corner, spoke quickly and guided Mara back to the room, sitting her on the bed, which had now been elevated on one side to support her back. Her body sagged and her eyes were having difficulty focusing. One man looked at the displays below her line of sight. The other opened a drawer and soon produced a small container of a thick liquid.

"Drink this, and it will help you will feel better." The man started to hold it to her lips in an effort to assist, but she took the container, alarmed that she was unable to control her shaky hand, but managed without help and without question. She rolled the liquid over her tongue before swallowing. *A strawberry flavor with a strange aftertaste.*

"I am Dr. Tanak," said the stocky man with beautiful olive skin. Something was a little different about him, but she could not concentrate enough to decide what it was.

"This is my friend, Officer Krey." A nice looking, taller man with a serious expression was watching her intently. She looked over to the doctor, with his reassuring countenance, but her eyes were drawn back to the officer. His face reflected such a thoughtful expression, she assumed there must be a problem. Then, he slowly smiled a most appealing smile, fading his somber appearance and revealing empathy and kindness. The broad shoulders and muscular build of these men were in high contrast to her previous acquaintances. Their better tailored clothing suggested higher status than the first she had encountered.

The drink had calmed her shakiness, but drowsiness was creeping through her. She rested her head back, and the bed reclined slowly.

"Sleep," Dr. Tanak said, "and you'll feel much better when you wake."

She remembered nothing else until she awoke with no sense of time, wondering how long she had been asleep. A small tray was perched on a narrow table beside her bed. A container of water, which her dry mouth craved, and another with a syrupy drink, beckoned. She took the water, sipping slowly at first, then gulping the last two swallows. Her still foggy mind was unwilling to maintain much thought, but her body felt stronger. She picked up the second container and sipped the same strawberry flavored drink she had previously been offered. The drink vessels were intriguing and required a closer inspection. They were made of a gray metallic material which looked to be of the same substance as the hall beams, but she did not recognize its composition. They seemed extremely light weight when compared to their sturdy feel. She was deep in concentration, running her thumb along the smooth surface of one, when the door opened.

A smiling, narrow shouldered woman with short, blunt-cut hair entered. She was dressed in the same basic tan clothing as her first two acquaintances.

"Hello, Mara," she said in a friendly tone, "I am Cali, your Helper. I am here to help you become familiar with our personal room facilities. Are you able to stand?"

Mara nodded as she carefully swung her legs off the bed and stood. After a moment, she took a deep breath, nodded again at Cali, and said hopefully, "I think I'm okay."

An unnoticed door along the left wall opened silently. Cali led her into a tiny enclosure, which made the small room with the bed seem spacious by comparison. Only one person could stand inside, the other in the doorway.

"Here is a hand wash automatic, commode automatic and your body wash automatic. They are the same in all areas of our transport. You will wash now; please remove clothing and stand in the body wash automatic."

With an almost hypnotic passiveness, Mara removed her simple, one-piece covering and stepped into the wash area. Soft pulsations of warm water sprayed from several spigots; warm caressing droplets which soothed a confused body and awakened long deprived sensory neurons. She closed her eyes and rubbed her face as if trying to send this warmth deep into her body. As the water massaged her, she was unaware that it became briefly foamy with soap before rinsing with clear water. And then, as suddenly as it had started, the water shut off and warm air blew on her body. She was surprised by the brevity of the shower, but now felt fresher and more alert. Cali handed her a small towel and a bag with a long shoulder strap.

"Your personal objects are in here. You will need to use the skin item. Dress and come with me, please." She stacked a more fitted, light green, long-sleeved top; thin, black, form-fitted pants; under garments and soft, short boots on the narrow shelf over the hand wash.

Mara used the thin towel to finish drying, dressed as quickly as her slightly wobbly legs allowed, grabbed the shoulder bag and followed Cali down the hall into an elevator. Cali spoke, the door closed, and momentarily the door opened onto a wider corridor. Lighting brightened ahead of them as they walked down a narrower passageway to the right.

"This is your room," her Helper announced as a door opened. Mara was barely in the room when Cali, already turning to leave, said, "Have a nice day."

Mara stared after her before giving an automatic "thank you."

"You are welcome, goodbye," Cali replied in her laconic manner and left with the same slightly stiff gait as the first two men she met.

An examination of the room took just seconds. On the opposite wall was a single bed which took up the entire width of the room. A high window above the bed shed light on the mere cubicle's austerity. On her left, near the door, stood a narrow cabinet. The adjacent wall supported a built-in short counter with two drawers underneath, one shelf above, and one chair. She placed her bag on the bed next to a blanket and pillow and sat down to rest as she looked around, eventually leaning back and closing her eyes. She drifted in and out of sleep before finally forcing herself to wake and continue her inspection of the remaining and unopened door near the bed. She attempted to touch the dark inset bar on its surface, but as her hand was about to touch it, the door opened. *Ah, the personal room and another claustrophobic space built for elves.*

She climbed on the bed to look out of the high wide window, whose light now suggested a bright beautiful day. To her disappointment, she found an obscured translucent material which offered no view. *Interior room, with a light screen to mimic sunshine.* With nothing else to explore, she sat back on the bed and turned her attention to the contents of her bag.

She pulled out two neatly folded identical long-sleeved light green tops with her name near the right shoulder, the thin black pants, foot coverings, under garments, a sleep set, and some random hygiene and grooming products. She opened a container which seemed to be lotion, applied a few drops to her arms and was mildly disturbed to see flakes of skin peeling off.   She put that aside to investigate an unusual hair care item which had three rows of wide-toothed combs. Not quite a comb, not quite a brush, but the word "comber" was on the handle, causing her to touch her still damp hair. No mirror in this space, and she felt no desire to find one, so she sat and combed her dark hair straight to her shoulders. She stared at the wall in front of her, suddenly feeling drained and empty and not knowing why.

2

Dr. Tanak and Officer Krey spoke freely as they walked.

"This one is interesting, but has me more than a little worried," Tanak confided. "First of all, I also don't understand why her rest pod opened. And then, waking up before the others and walking out without help. This shouldn't have happened. We've just started reducing the medications in her group the same as we've done in the past, with no problems with any of the others. Now, she's awake and has received none of the meds to help with her memory transfers, and those have to be given before they wake up." The concern in his voice was palpable when he continued.

"Her scans always looked good, but I'm running a review of all her records in case there was a problem with her protocol. Now that she's awake, we'll need to be closely monitoring brain function, particularly the prefrontal cortex of her brain, for any unusual emotional responses. The last thing we need is some strange outbursts or a major bout of depression. Some of the reactions to the long inert stage without the medications can lead to extreme mood and emotional swings. Have you noticed anything we should be concerned about?"

Krey walked a few steps before answering. He always entrusted the brain function material to Tanak's expertise. His chief concern would be how well she could assimilate and be productive in a totally new environment, and for that he would need time with her.

"I know that the rest pod is being checked for any malfunction. It's still a mystery as to why it initiated a complete shutdown sequence so early. But, as far as she goes, there is nothing that I could see in a cursory look at her records anyway. I'd have to see her in person a few more times before I could offer any educated opinion. She must have a strong system, well educated, seems compliant and steady considering all, certainly nice looking. Ratings must have been high or she wouldn't have been accepted." Tanak raised his thin eyebrows and gave a sidelong glance at his overly serious colleague.

"Are you interested in her? That's a first for you in a while."

"I'm not sure, but she definitely intrigues me." A rare smile crossed his face. "I do want to take another closer look at her records and talk to her, and find out if we overlooked anything."

Arriving at the door, Krey gave a couple soft knocks, opened it, and they entered the room to see Mara sitting with a blank look on her face. *She looks so forlorn. Is she going to cry?* He hadn't seen crying in a long while.

Tanak tried to give an extra cheerful hello, and she returned a reflexive faint smile.

"We're checking in to see how you are feeling and do a little checkup. Were you experiencing any pain or soreness?" He took a small cylindrical instrument from his pocket and moved it near her head and chest. He looked at Krey and gave an okay nod.

"No, just a little unsteady, but I think better now." And then she suddenly added, "I think I'm lost. I can't remember where I am."

Both men quickly make eye contact with each other, while she looked at Krey with a pleading expression.

"Am I on a ship?"

He hesitated before answering. "Yes, and we're taking you home."

He was relieved when she seemed to accept this brief explanation.

To distract her, he added, "Let me show you around a little if you feel strong enough. Do you feel up to going for a short walk?"

She could produce no opinion or care if she went or not, but her dull state of mind nodded obligingly. She stood up, and her comber, forgotten in her lap, began to slip. She grabbed it and attempted to put it up on the shelf over the counter, but it escaped her grasp. As it fell, she noticed something inexplicable to her foggy brain. The comber did not fall straight down, but rather fell ever so slightly to her right in an almost imperceptible curve. She could not place what it was that bothered her about this, so she just stared at it and then at Krey. He stared back for a moment, and no one spoke.

He then bent down and picked up the comber, placed it on the shelf and said, perfectly normally, "Let me know if you get too tired, and we'll come right back."

They walked out in the hall, while he led the conversation with any inane topic which came to mind. They slowly continued to a wider area which spilt into two corridors, where they encountered a few people in similar uniforms who passed them with perfunctory glances. Two men then approached with leering stares, which made Mara feel uncomfortable enough to instinctively move closer to Krey until her shoulder was touching his arm. The men grinned at Krey, and he returned a cool nod with a solemn face. He sensed Mara's uneasiness and diverted her attention.

"If you turn at this blue wall, you will come to a dining area."

Through a wide doorway, they entered a pleasant space with several tables able to seat two, four or six diners. There was a narrow rectangular shaped area filled with artificial plants in the middle of the room, creating an ambiance which suggested some privacy between tables. Two tables were occupied, and the diners stopped and looked up briefly before continuing their conversations.

"For a while, I think it will be better if you eat in your room. When you feel stronger, we'll have you venture out more."

She admitted that she wasn't feeling like herself and made no complaints when he returned her to her room where a small meal awaited. When she was alone, she surveyed the neatly arranged tray which held another small container of water, a gray metallic plate with a square piece of something of undetermined origin, and a container of a pudding type substance. Although the portions were small, the amount of food seemed to match her level of hunger. The taste was satisfactory, although she could not determine the genesis of the brown square and was surprised to find that the pudding was not sweet, but savory.

After eating, she put her few belongings in the drawers and the cabinet. In one drawer she was pleased to find an intelligent reader which opened at her touch. She spent over an hour exploring its contents of reading material and brain games before a deep sleep overcame her.

3

It took almost another full day for Mara's mind to address the door's function. Cali had just delivered her food tray and was leaving when Mara realized that the door closed automatically. Her Helper hadn't touched it; the door merely closed deliberately and solidly when she left, which was not uncommon, but its thick metal composition drew attention, reminding her of the hall ceiling beam material and seeming unnecessarily thick for such a small room. Her vague reasoning allowed her to rationalize the sturdy door as a safety barrier in case of a water breach. She got up and walked to the exact spot where Cali was standing when she was about to leave, and, yes, the door silently began opening. She stepped back into the room and it closed. This seemingly important revelation was stored for future use, because she could force no desire to go anywhere.

For the next few days her calm state of mind and fragile physical strength relished a quiet routine. The mornings always began with a very brief shower, and she was relieved when her skin stopped peeling with the help of the lotion Cali had suggested. Her body was gradually getting stronger, aided no doubt with many hours of sleep, but her mind was still strangely quiet and acquiescent.

At the first sound of a very soft brushing on her door's exterior, she opened it to find a durable rectangle with two eyes and an endearing graphic of a smile. Two large, vertically rotating rollers were cleaning the bottom four feet of the wall, and she could see a quickly drying lane on the floor where it had passed. The faint redolence of disinfectant filled the hall.

In her surprise she asked, without expecting an answer, "Well hello, who are you?"

It stopped, and she guessed it was identifying her through its camera eyes. It answered in a rather cartoon voice.

"Hello Mara. I am Mopmop. I am here to clean your hall. Mopmop loves to clean."

She couldn't help being amused.

"Nice to meet you Mopmop. Don't let me interrupt you. Keep on cleaning."

As the robot moved down the hall, she heard it repeat, "Mopmop loves to clean."

A few mornings later, she heard the Mopmop remain outside her door. She opened the door fully expecting to encounter some kind of mechanical problem.

The robot was facing the door and said, "Hello Mara. Today is clothes cleaning day. Please give Mopmop clothes to clean."

A top latch released, revealing an empty compartment while Mopmop stayed and waited. Mara gathered some of her clothes, lifted the unlatched lid and dumped the wadded-up bundle inside. Mopmop said "thank you", turned and continued down the hall, leaving Mara to wonder if she would ever see her clothes again. The worries were proven groundless when Cali arrived after dinner with a neatly folded pile of clean clothes.

When her eyes opened the next morning, she lay still, staring at the faux window, watching it slowly brighten to simulate sunrise. She wished she could remember dreams. Other people remembered dreams, and she imagined those memories would be like having exciting experiences. A sound of talking startled her daydreaming into the present. A video had spontaneously appeared on the wall, and she became mesmerized at the menu of choices to view. Video clips pertaining to health, the various jobs performed on the ship, or brief documentaries about a person's work in a science or math field. Most often, they were associated with physical fitness, stretching or cardio routines, usually only 15 or 20 minutes long, but Mara knew she would follow along in her limited space, grateful for the diversion.

Throughout the next day, she felt a growing, pent-up energy with no outlet. Trying to engage Cali in a stimulating conversation proved futile. She was highly efficient at her assigned duties but seemed uninterested in any pleasant dialogue. Mara paced the tiny room, did an exercise routine, and paced again with only growing frustration of not having enough to occupy her ever more alert mind. She walked into the hallway, quiet, empty and stark, and returned to her room with higher agitation. Her breathing quickened with a need to escape the boredom; anxiety was washing over her when she heard a unique tone emanating from her intelligent reader.

Upon inspection, she found several electronic music selections, new stories, articles, and two novels. She flipped through the titles with the happy anticipation of someone about to start a vacation. From the first story pages, her small cubicle expanded through the world of words. The walls faded away while her curious and empathetic thoughts met characters and traveled vicariously on new explorations. Her mind became stimulated, her thinking focused as she was transported on adventures and emotional journeys. She sat and read, or let her reader narrate the story while she relaxed on her bed as if on a magic carpet, letting her mind envision the story unfolding before her.

Despite these new interests and her increased alertness, her enigmatic mind remained strangely accepting of the present moment, giving little thought of the past or future. She passed the routine days in her limited world, always waiting with anticipation for the taps on the door, for the visits from her new friends who could enrich her life.

4

The highlights of her days were always the visits from Dr. Tanak and Officer Krey, which never failed to lift her spirits.

"No formalities," they had told her, "It's just Tanak and Krey to you."

Tanak checked her health and strength which seemed to improve slowly each day, even though she seemed to be sleeping an inordinate amount of time.

"Sleep is very good for you now, don't fight it," he would say reassuringly. "You're doing remarkably well."

Her mind and body assessments often included tasks: some puzzles, spatial or logic tasks, at first on her reader, and later on an air projection, where the format was greatly enlarged. It didn't matter what the task was, she simply enjoyed the mental stimulation and the company, which always produced outward smiles and inward happiness. The men responded with generic comments on her performance, sometimes with a "thank you," or "nicely done," always accompanied by an encouraging smile.

The differences in the men became more apparent each time they visited. Tanak had a face and mannerisms which projected assurance and confidence. At first, she found it difficult not to stare at the thin ridge on his forehead, on which grew thin eyebrows that all but connected above his nose. The ridge produced the effect of making his eyes appear to be set deeper into his face. The lobes of his ears were thin and close to his head, and the closely cut dark hair on the sides of his head made them more noticeable. The longer hair on the top of his head was combed to one side in a failed attempt to lead the eye away from the brow line. Thankfully, his unique features produced fewer distractions as she became more accustomed to his appearance.

Krey, the quiet one, was normal in appearance, she decided, quite handsome in a rugged sort of way, with his light brown hair, grayish green eyes and an agreeable smile, when it crossed his normally serious face. With a furtive, but admiring gaze, she noticed that he wore his uniform well. She could tell both men liked and respected each other by their informal speech and collegial demeanor when interacting.

Krey, she observed, was beginning to find time to drop in on his own, and she found herself looking forward to his visits. He noticed her attentive manner and sensed her enjoyment in their meetings. He admitted to himself that he was attracted to her appearance, the shiny, straight, dark hair that framed a pretty face, the nicely shaped, trim body. It was easy for him to rationalize the time spent with her, telling himself it helped to analyze how she was adjusting to the new environment.

Time together was normally spent on short walks, allowing her to become familiar with limited areas of the ship. They met more people who looked normal to her and a few who seemed narrow shouldered and thin. When she remarked on their appearance, he paused briefly before answering.

"They are our AI technicians, or Helpers, as we call them. We have several on board to work on the ship, which allows us to use less human crew members. They're programmed for specific jobs, and they don't stress our food or water supplies"

Mara said nothing as she processed this information, thinking about how many she had seen on board and how it explained Cali's condensed speech.

"Exactly, where are we?" she asked.

He gave her a quick glance while trying to determine the best response, and finally managed to say, "We're not actually anywhere specific at the moment, but we'll be home in a relatively short time." Then he quickly added, "Come, I want to show you something special."

They turned into a new passageway and continued walking until he stopped and gave two short whistles. A medium sized dog trotted out of a nearby door, stopped momentarily and then came bounding up to greet them. Mara's surprised expression transformed into delight up as she knelt down.

"Hey, come here, buddy."

She has a beautiful smile, Krey thought, as the dog came up and received Mara's undivided attention. As she was petting it, her expression changed, and she looked up questioningly.

"What is this?" The dog ignored her question, wagging his tail and panting with a happy expression on its face.

"It's one of our AI pets. We can't maintain real animals on long voyages, but these become easy in our minds to take their place. His artificial intelligence will surprise you and win you over. You'll see."

The dog's appearance and behavior were very convincing, and if it hadn't been for its slightly firmer body, it would have taken her longer to decipher the truth. His happy expression was enhanced by one ear which flopped forward. He nuzzled her for more attention, which she gladly gave.

"What's his name?" she asked.

"I think we should call him Buddy." He answered. "Would you like to keep him for a while?"

She was kneeling on the floor, sitting on her heels with an arm around the dog, when she looked up and smiled at him. "Yes, very much."

Their eyes met, and she realized how much her affection for this man was growing. She enjoyed the visits from Tanak, but it was Krey who lightened her heart. He turned, looked at the pet, and then spoke a brief sequence of numbers. Suddenly, the AI dog stood completely still until Krey said, "Buddy."

"He will come to his name now, and knows all the basic dog commands, sit, stay and all, and more. I'll send Cali over later to give you more instructions." He walked her back to her room, leaving her to get acquainted with Buddy.

She sat on her bed, and the dog sat and looked up at her with a tongue-out smile. He, she decided it was a he, had very authentic feeling short, golden fur with enough white around its neck to look like a wide collar, and some white shown on the tip of the tail.

"You are a mutt, but they definitely put a little collie or lab in your nice face." Buddy stared and gave a tail wag. She was wondering how long it would stare at her when Cali knocked and entered. Buddy turned quickly to face her as she put a metal board on the ground near the wall.

"Greetings. This is AI 7-D's charging station, where it will dock at night. Areas of the ship are equipped for continuous D charging, but that is not in this room. AI 7-D knows 279 words and phrases in your language. Search AI 7-D in your intelligent reader, and you will learn about this pet. Have a nice day."

She turned in her businesslike manner and walked away.

The next hour was spent immersed in her reader, asking about Buddy. She practiced the basic dog obedience commands with him, then moved on to having him retrieve objects and play tug of war, which revealed his considerable strength. The information mentioned that the intuitive mode was on.

"I'll bet you can learn more words as we get to know each other."

Buddy put a paw on her knee. The numerous ways he mimicked a real dog were uncanny. He projected happiness in a furry package of wagging, wiggling and panting, and she was beginning to understand how people could easily begin to think of this as a live dog.

5

Captain Lor, Dr. Tanak, and Chief Officer Krey were engaged in amiable conversations while finishing up a quick lunch in the compact officers' dining area. Here were the big three of the ship, who met through their work but soon became friends. Friendships were always an added bonus, when a good rapport not only enriched the time on board, but became a necessity on long transport missions in confined spaces.

"I don't know how, but I can just perceive by the rhythm of the work and the atmosphere on board, that everyone can sense we're well over the half way mark home," Tanak said. "It's already time to start the wakeups tomorrow. It seems to be a very successful mission, if Mara is any indication of the quality of passengers we have picked up. We'll keep the same schedule as the previous expedition and awaken them in groups of five every two days until all 55 are ready for departure when we dock."

Tanak, a Creo-human, was head physician in charge of overseeing the evaluation, selection and care for all the new passengers. He and his small elite team were knowledgeable in the anatomy and health of the two classes of humans. This important job assured their home of future generations. He was single; the bond with his wife had failed, no doubt in part due to long work separations which took a toll on partnerships. He'd had a few short-term relationships, but was leery of making another commitment. He was enjoying his job, he always said, and didn't need any more drama in his life.

"I hope everyone works out well. I'm not sure if we'll ever travel back there again," Lor stated. "We've been very fortunate on this trip in terms of finding a direct path and keeping the voyage within a decent time period. I was hoping to be able to acquire more materials to expedite the upgrades to our shuttle transports. They're sadly out of date, but things seem like they've really deteriorated back home, and we were lucky to get the supplies we got."

Lor, an Alpha level IQ enhanced human, was the capable captain, having earned a reputation for his piloting and management skills on the two previous long voyage missions. His enhanced intelligence and experience working on various ships made him a veritable computer of knowledge about the workings of the craft. He was 47 years old, if anyone could figure out a reliable age on these types of trips. He often spoke of his family, and they knew he made electronic contact with his wife and nine–year-old daughter on the rare times home communication was available. Any data transmission at these distances entailed lengthy time delays and, despite advances in the technology, still consumed vast amounts of power.

Krey's mind was roaming off, thinking how interesting this trip had turned out with Mara awakening early, a first as far as he knew, on any trip. It gave him a rare chance to spend individual time with a new person, and he found himself thinking more about her and finding excuses to see her. He might even like to see her again when they got home. He was single and never felt he had the necessary time to invest in commitments to another, always blaming the importance of their work for the lack of a personal life. But thinking of Mara, he wondered, for the first time, if he wasn't ready for a more permanent relationship.

He was a Level Two IQ enhanced human and the transport and resource officer, making sure nothing interfered with the major mission of the voyage, safely transporting new inhabitants and procuring supplies. His brainpower and advanced knowledge of artificial intelligence, coupled with an intuitive personality, allowed him to successfully work with the numerous temperaments of crew and passengers, a most necessary skill on lengthy expeditions. He possessed an intense seriousness about his work, knowing that any technical malfunction or friction among crew members could become a major problem in a confined environment. This quality made him one of the most thorough and reliable members of the crew.

His thoughts were interrupted by Tanak, who continued the conversation.

"It definitely seemed more dangerous and difficult to find intelligent, qualified and drug free people this time. This could possibly be the last trip for who knows how long, and that doesn't bother me a bit. If there ever were another long voyage, I wouldn't be surprised if it would likely be into new uncharted territories."

They became quiet for a moment, thinking of their mind-bending travel. It had been an incredibly short journey by physics standards and, at the same time, a long journey by human standards, lasting almost three years. Traveling previously unfathomable distances became only possible by the continual probing, mapping and fine-tuning the structure of space, combined with the advances they had made in nuclear power and electromagnetic propulsion. They had made progress with quantum tunneling, but the conundrum of superluminal motion, moving faster than the speed of light, the holy grail of long voyage travel, still just evaded them. They were grateful for an untold number of physicists, mathematicians, the centuries of work, and a good degree of luck for getting them where they were. In human terms, however, this often seemed like a long voyage for the crew, who were happily anticipating getting off the confined space of the ship and back to home port until their next assignment.

Lor broke the silence. "I'm thinking of having a union bonding ceremony before we dock. Or a life alliance, a bonding pact, a life agreement, whatever the heck we're supposed to call it now. I've heard talk that several crew members joined this mission because they assumed there would be a ceremony before we got home, and now I think most of the crew seems to expect it. That is, Tanak, if you think the Candidates seem adjusted well enough."

"We'll know soon enough," said Tanak, "It's understandable that the crew would hope for the ceremony. It gives them first choice before the new ones join the rest of society, and it's some compensation for this long tour. All of the Candidates' scans look good, and they should adjust well."

Krey was quiet, his fingers tapping his mug, looking at the wall across the room with a wistful smile, his mind back to thinking of Mara. He hadn't known Lor was thinking of a life bonding rite. Tanak was studying him with a lopsided grin. He did not quite recognize the smile on his normally serious friend's face. Something or someone was affecting him in a positive way, and the only thought to which he could attribute this change was Mara.

"Anyone in the data look interesting to our confirmed loner?" Lor asked, looking at Krey.

"He seems to be spending all of his spare time with the early riser," Tanak answered for him. "He even has an AI dog with her now."

"Is that right? Probably a veritable expert on her." Lor was grinning now. "See any problems with her? This early wake-up is a new one for me. Should we be worried?"

Krey ignored the good-natured jabs and said, "She's asking more questions than usual, but satisfied with basic answers for now. She's very observant, even noticed the spin gravity shift in a falling object soon after she woke up. Intelligent, should be good." More than good, he thought, as they got up to return to their positions.

6

Mara's room was shrinking in its confinement. With each day, her once dormant mind gained clarity, her body strengthened, and she yearned for more stimulation. A walk or run on the outdoor deck would be wonderfully refreshing, but that was never mentioned, and she intuitively sensed that she should not ask to go outside. She ventured out of her room every day now with Buddy as her constant companion, going to the limited areas she recognized from her walks with Krey.

In the middle of the day, she would sometimes wander through the halls with Buddy, her reader in hand, and sit in the corner of the dining area, hungry only for a change of scenery. More Helpers began showing up in her section of the ship. She always greeted them with her ready smiles and friendly hellos, and although they all recognized her and replied, they never stopped to talk, remaining dutifully focused on their assigned tasks.

Her mind had mapped out her limited hallways, originally as confusing as twisted branches of an overgrown tree, but now filed under routines and taking no concentration to navigate. The familiar passageways widened whenever there was a connecting hall, and all had similar curved gray beams. The bottom half of the walls, the part Mopmop cleaned, varied in muted colors, helping her to remember the maze of halls and the route back to her room.

She was forced to redirect her walks whenever she came to an inaccessible door. She would try standing in different places in front of the barrier, but it would never release until she would admit defeat and go back to familiar areas.

On one singular occasion, she was able to follow a crew member through one of the doors before it closed. She began to explore the new area, but within seconds a Helper appeared.

"Hello Mara. This is a restricted section for working crew members. I will escort you back to the area open to passengers." He was wearing a fixed smile, looking straight at her with an unwavering stare and waiting. Perceiving no alternative, she turned and followed when she sensed the futility of not complying. It was not long after that she began to occasionally see other men or women dressed in clothing similar to hers, accompanied by a Helper, but never stopping to talk.

Her most frequent forays were to a room with a few pieces of exercise equipment. She enjoyed her routine on each unit, gradually adding more repetitions, and the occasional sore muscles were worth the shortness of breath she experienced on exertion. At times, someone would look in and quickly leave once they saw her.

One afternoon, however, while she was working on an adaptive trainer, she saw Buddy whirl and look toward the door. She turned to see the two men who had previously made her feel uncomfortable. They had the same creepy grins, causing her to feel uneasy and wishing there was another way out of the room.

"Well, look who's here. And she rates an AI-D?"

Mara moved closer to Buddy as she read the name Dren on the shirt of the arrogant speaker. He started toward her while tinges of fear began coloring her mind.

"Buddy, alert," she said. Buddy stood with ears forward and growled.

The second man, Draven, laughed.

"That AI won't hurt a human. Didn't they tell you that?" He moved toward her, grabbing her arm.

"Buddy, guard," Mara commanded. Buddy began a low barking sound which increased in volume.

"Shut that thing up," Dren ordered, as he came toward Buddy with a kick that knocked him over. Buddy righted himself and kept up his barking at a now near deafening level. Rapid footsteps approached.

A tall, sturdy man entered, spoke in an indecipherable tone, and the barking ceased. He glared at the men with narrow eyes.

"You are dismissed. Report to Conduct." His imposing face and posture reflected such disapproval that Mara was surprised when Draven dared to object.

"We only wanted to speak with her, and she alerted that AI pet."

The man turned as if to ask Mara, but seeing her distressed face, repeated to the men in an even more authoritative voice, "Report to conduct."

Dren, so sure of himself a minute ago, was the first to leave the room.

The man looked briefly toward Mara. "Are you going to be okay now?"

She nodded, but before she could speak, he turned and walked away with the men.

"Come on, Buddy, we're going back to our room." She found herself shaking with a combination of anger and adrenalin. Her agitation continued, shaking her head and hands as if she were trying to rid herself of the upsetting experience and the jolting, piercing barks, which had shattered the ship's normal low hums.

Hearing her name, she turned and was relieved to see Krey walking determinedly toward her. He came up and instinctively put his arm around her and guided her toward her quarters. She leaned against him and, without thinking, put her arm around his waist for moral support. It had been a while since he had felt a woman's touch. He brought her closer, and they walked without speaking.

"Buddy, dock," Krey ordered when they entered Mara's room. Buddy immediately reclined on his docking station, becoming completely immobile with eyes closed.

They sat down on her bed, and he kept his arm around her shoulders in an effort to calm her unsettling experience. She rested her head against him and neither spoke. The muscles in his neck and shoulders tightened, his mind disturbed with inscrutable thoughts and emotions. He was supposed to be the steady officer, but his contemplations only produced raw anger at the men who bothered Mara and disappointment in the stupidity of their brash behavior. He wondered if he had missed something which should have warned him of their lapse of judgement. Mostly, he felt the strong need to protect her.

As her pounding heart quieted and her unraveled nerves began to reset, Mara became aware of his closeness, with his arm still around her, his hand resting on her shoulder. The sensual feelings it evoked surprised her. She kept her head against him, breathing in the moment. In that instant, she loved her uninspiring room for momentarily insulating them in this shell of solitude.

"They won't bother you again," he finally said when he could trust himself to sound like an officer in control. She looked at him and, when their eyes met, they both felt that some inexplicable, very personal sentiment had passed between them. Neither spoke, so absorbed were they both in the emotion, making it all the stronger. He had the fleeting thought of kissing her, stopping only by quickly standing and taking her hand.

"Would you like to see my favorite spot on this whole ship?"

7

They walked down the hall, making two turns before coming to a door.

"This ascender is currently open only to Level 3 crew." He raised the palm of his hand toward the wall, the door opened, they entered, and he said "Level Dome." The door closed and a moment later he said, "Now close your eyes."

He led her out of the ascender, but before she could even open her eyes, her olfactory organs exploded with the revitalizing smells of the outdoors. Her eyes widened and her mouth parted in astonishment as she beheld a wonderland scene of evergreens, ferns, and a trail. Euphoria filled her mind as her senses were overwhelmed with sights of rich hues, and sounds of birds and water. Her eyes swept over the scene, searching for their origins. Krey watched them fill with tears as she breathed in deeply, as if to inhale the richness of this experience into her soul. To her left, she found a small waterfall emptying into a shallow pond.

She caught her breath in surprise. "Look at these fish!" she exclaimed, peering into the water. There were beautiful fish of varying sizes, speckled light and dark green, all swimming through water clear enough to see pebbles below.

"They're so amazing!" she said as she moved her hand through the cool water. Then, she stopped abruptly, looked up and asked, "Are these real?"

"Oh sure, very real. They're here for their beauty and for this experimental micro ecosystem, but we farm other fish at home for fresh food."

She looked at him quizzically. "But the ocean…" she started to say, but a bird trill interrupted her thought. A small, intensely colored, yellow and black bird darted into the foliage above her. Mara laughed and started on the trail. It wound around narrow turns, up and down gentle slopes until they came to a rustic bench nearly engulfed in shrubbery.

"This is where I come sometimes," he said as they sat, "when I just want to listen to the peaceful sounds of nature. It refreshes my mind."

"It's beautiful," she answered softly, smiling, looking up, lost in thought.

A distinct waft of pine scent drifted to her, and an unexpected memory of walking through a forest raced in and out of her mind. She caught her breath in surprise.

"Are you okay?" he asked, concerned.

"I thought I remembered something, but it's gone now." She was staring, concentrating to recall the phantom image, now lost.

"We'd better get back," he said as he stood. They meandered back, not talking as she looked everywhere, taking deep breaths, touching leaves. She smiled at him, a smile that filled him with pleasure.

The exit from the dome was jarring. To leave an area full of deep colors, scents, and life to enter a stark hall of straight, smooth surfaces and sharp angles was a like a jolt to the brain. She was quiet on the way back, trying to cement images into her memory, which seemed to be clawing at recollections just out of reach.

When he dropped her off at her room, she said, "Thank you, I loved it. I hope we can visit there again."

"We definitely will someday," he promised.

8

The following day, Mara was quietly enjoying a story on her reader and talking absently to Buddy when there was a knock at the door.

Cali entered saying, "You will dine with others from now on. Please follow me."

Finally. Time would have passed so slowly without Krey's visits. She could barely remember her first days here, and they all seemed to merge together, making it difficult for her to determine how much time had passed. Even though she had Cali and Buddy, she found herself happy to have even a visit from Mopmop, who occasionally stopped to pick up her laundry. She knew she was craving and ready for more social interaction and new experiences. Cali led her to the dining room by the blue wall, where she saw other young women moving through a line to receive a tray of food.

"You may get your food. Enjoy your dinner," Cali said, already moving away.

The line moved steadily as the nine identically dressed women picked up trays and wandered hesitantly to tables. Mara took her dinner, sat at an empty table for two and scanned the room. The women were of different nationalities and skin tones, all almost too thin, and all with almost the same length hair as her own. She watched them for a moment, wondering if she would be able to understand any of them.

She turned her attention to her meal of a small protein, vegetables, and exactly four pieces of small, delicate looking lettuce leaves. A citrus aroma floated up from the meager salad, causing her to fixate on the refreshingly pungent smell. She was resisting the urge to put her nose near her plate for a deep inhale when a woman sat across from her.

"Hello," she said in a quiet, but friendly voice.

Mara smiled at her, "Hi. I'm Mara."

"They call me Genna." A pretty, auburn haired woman with a fair, almost porcelain complexion, returned the smile. She hesitated as if she wanted to say something, but changed her mind and began nibbling at her food.

"Have you met any of the other women?" asked Mara.

"No, this is my first night with others. I'm feeling a little unsure of all this right now, still trying to clear my head, I guess. I'm afraid I don't feel very hungry, and I can't tell what this is," she said, pointing to the protein square with an amused chuckle.

"I know." Mara stabbed the square with her fork and waved it in the air. "I am your tasty little cardboard dinner," she said in a high voice, making Genna laugh again.

Then in her normal voice she added, "I don't know what it is either, but it surprisingly satisfies hunger. Eat a little, rest, and you'll feel better tomorrow," giving Genna the same advice Tanak had given her.

The room had remained eerily quiet as everyone was subdued, trying to assess the room without being too obvious. Genna's laughter seemed to lighten the mood, and small conversations were tentatively starting, but never seemed to fully develop. The dinner progressed quickly, and as soon as she finished, Mara stood up to take her tray to a cleaning shelf and return to her room.

"I guess I'll see you tomorrow. Get some sleep tonight." She could already tell she was going to be good friends with this woman. It was like meeting someone and immediately feeling a comfortable connection and knowing that shared interests would be found.

Genna nodded and gave her a thumbs-up sign with a warm smile. "Great, I'll see you then."

Mara entered her room, filled with elation at the prospect of new acquaintances. Flopping on the bed and staring up at the drab ceiling, she told Buddy about eating in the dining room with the new women.

"More people to talk to, Buddy. That means more friends, not that I don't appreciate you, but I mean, I was actual getting happy to see Mopmop for a distraction, and I need something more to keep my mind busy." She looked at the AI pet, which was looking at her with a tilted head as if he understood.

"I don't know why I talk to you, except I know you're my captive audience, and I guess if you weren't here, I might be talking to myself."

Buddy wagged his tail and sat close to her. She wondered how long she could keep him now that new people were around.

As the following days progressed, the young women became acquainted; their placid personalities remained as their bodies slowly strengthened. Several of the new travelers now shared rooms near Mara and were sometimes seen in the hall accompanied by a Helper or walking with a crew member. Grateful now to have her own small room, she found it hard to imagine having to share the cramped space with another.

Other men and women were occasionally seen passing in hallways, but her group interactions were always with the nine women she had first seen in the dining area. The tone of the newly awakened groups remained subdued, even though all seemed compatible and pleasant. All were kept busy working on aptitude assessments, learning about ship information and communications devices.

It was not long before they were introduced to the AI pets, and Buddy had to return to the community group, although Mara still felt surprisingly attached to this inanimate being. Three other AI -Ds and two AI -Cs were introduced to the group. Two small dogs and a medium sized one joined Buddy. Each had distinctive personalities, which somehow seemed in harmony with the different personalities of the young women. The small gray dog was hyperactive, the brown one was calmly inquisitive, and the white one with pale tan spots on its back seemed easy going. One thin, very sociable cat, with black with white markings on its face and legs, loved all the attention. The fat, rust-colored cat raced erratically around the area for no apparent reason, earning the name Turbo. It displayed a very disinterested and unpredictable personality, often looking deceptively friendly before swishing its tail angrily if someone tried to pet it.

The AI pets were good ice breakers and had the desired effect of getting the quiet group of women to talk more together. The amusing antics, with the near perfect imitations of animal behaviors, produced the desired laughter and cheerfulness as they interacted with everyone. From then on, the pets often were found in various areas, performing delivery tasks, accompanying a person, or immobile, waiting for a command. Turbo was randomly seen wandering the halls carrying a cloth rat, and no one dared disturb it. Buddy was still often seen with Mara, as if somehow, everyone thought of him as her pet.

She enjoyed meeting and interacting with the new Candidates, as they were called. Her easy laugh and friendly self-confidence made her well liked with the new travelers. They continued to see more new men and women, now and then, but her group never changed. The men, all dressed in their black pants and dark green shirts, lived in another area, but often joined the women for meals or classes.

Work schedules soon appeared on Candidates' intelligent readers. In small increments, everyone was assigned a job, creating a set program which kept the newly awakened travelers occupied for most of the day. Everyone trained and helped at a job for a few days before rotating to a new position. They were not expected to master any task in such a short time, but were monitored to observe any special skills or talents and to see how quickly they adapted to change and new information. The jobs varied from hydroponic gardening, medical clinic training, air and water filtration monitoring, to basic cleaning and AI maintenance. Everyone was busy, with their minds occupied learning new information and adjusting to the new tasks.

Although there were many areas of the ship that were unexplored and off limits to Candidates, they did have an added bonus with the introduction to one of the mini pod stores which occasionally appeared near the dining area or in a hallway junction. With work credits they could purchase personal miscellaneous goods from a small selection of flavored drinks, jewelry, hair accessories, or games and stories for their readers, all of which seemed popular.

The one item in the pod store which continued to attract Mara's attention was a necklace with a single star shining with a luminescent quality. The star hung from a single metal strand which made a flowing loop down each side above the star before encircling and holding its two arm points. The shining points were unadorned except for the artistically formed metal wire. Something in its simplicity and sheen kept strangely calling to her. When she had enough credits, she purchased it and, from that time, was never seen without it.

9

The second visit with Krey to the outdoor dome found Mara more prepared for a closer inspection of the area. The trees, grown on raised platforms to appear taller than their relatively short stature, weren't as numerous as they originally seemed. She noticed a few columbines and other plants mixed in with the ferns, and she caught the movement of a small nuthatch on a tree trunk.

The size of this green oasis was much smaller than its first impression. The winding trail was essentially very tightly curved with thick foliage between, giving the illusion of greater distance. She now guessed that the sky must be artificial light giving an impression of a sunlit sky. Despite this realization, the presence of the wondrous living species still uplifted her spirit and brought her an inner gladness. Krey watched her closely, saw the joyful quietness of her demeanor and contemplated whether he should show her to another area of the ship.

On the way back to a common area, he made his decision.

"There is one more special area I want to show you. It is open day and night to any crew member who wishes to visit."

Her curiosity rose as she never thought about anything being open during the night. They took a narrow mover to a section called Meditation and entered a beautiful room with walls appearing to be half wooden. There were two beautifully crafted stained-glass windows flanking three tall plants in a large planter. This foliage appeared alive and growing, if their varying sized leaves were any indication. There were only a few chairs scattered throughout the room and two short rows of padded chairs with kneelers. She saw small religious symbols decorating the walls and thought she recognized a crucifix, a crescent and star, and the dharma wheel. She gravitated toward the crucifix and sat down, and Krey carefully moved a chair over and sat next to her. After a few moments she closed her eyes, and he wondered at her thoughts.

He was looking intently at her when she opened her eyes, turned toward him and asked, "This is your church?"

"Well, in a way, yes," he said in a quiet voice, "more of a multi-denominational area, where travelers are invited to pray and meditate or just enjoy the silence."

She studied his face.

"Do you ever come here?"

"Yes," he answered, "there are many times it brings me comfort to be still, think and believe there is a power greater than man. My initial training is in science, but I've found that sometimes, after you've exhausted all the science you can explore, all you have left to explain some things is the mystery of your God."

He paused with a gaze of one whose thoughts momentarily drifted afar, then shook his head slightly before adding, "The complexities of the universe are absolutely mind boggling."

He shrugged and gave a reflective smile.

"I guess I can thank Tanak for making me realize that it's important to nurture both my physical and spiritual being. Tanak's faith is so strong it sometimes seems to cover and become infused in me when I'm with him. Somehow, I find that comforting, especially when I see what a good man he is."

She was studying his face, realizing he was revealing some very personal thoughts, and it pleased her that he would share them with her. She gave a slight nod with a serene and understanding expression, thinking how that may explain Tanak's ability to always convey an assurance that all things were under control.

"May I come here sometime?"

"Of course," he said, happy in his decision to bring her here. "Just remember this is considered a quiet area. If anyone says anything to you, just tell them I brought you here. It's currently open only to crew members, but soon will be open to all travelers. Now, let me show you the way back so you don't get lost."

Later, when she visited a few times after her work assignment, she found others sitting or kneeling quietly. Formal prayers escaped her, so she silently thought about her gratefulness or concerns. Her concerns were always related to her mind, which was sharp and quick in many ways, yet the indefinable memories were still hidden in locked chambers filled with evasive sections of her life. She was grateful for so much: her new friends, Tanak, who was so knowledgeable and supportive, her Helper Cali, and mostly for Krey, the caring man who never failed to lift her spirits. Her time at Meditation always calmed her mind, especially now that Tanak and Krey's visits were becoming less frequent.

She saw them now only occasionally down a hall or across a room working with the new people. She missed them both, but especially Krey. She always looked for him, and at times, they would catch each other's eyes from across a room or down a hall and smile. He seemed very busy now, and there seemed to be a higher tension in the air displayed by the elevated activity from the crew.

One late afternoon, Mara was in an exercise room with Genna and a striking Asian woman named Omi. All the women seemed to have affable personalities, but she especially enjoyed the company of these two, with whom she often worked. She was putting some weights down when she noticed Dren and Draven watching from the door. The other women ignored them and kept on exercising. She glared at the men, wishing Buddy were here, when they mumbled something to each other before Draven looked at her and said, "Soon."

They both laughed in what Mara thought was a rather malicious way, and then walked away leaving her with a disconcerted stare and wondering what Draven meant by his one-word statement.

On her way back to her quarters, she was surprised to see several crew members huddled around two illuminated areas on the hallway walls. She paused, watching how they read and talked with interest about the postings. When they left, curiosity prompted her to see what seemed so important. Both screens now only displayed a graphic of stars with a long-tailed lightning bolt running across the screen. Minute, undecipherable writing was displayed on the tail of the lightning, hieroglyphics to her. As she stood there, the illumination faded and disappeared until she was staring at a blank wall. Shrugging her shoulders, she continued to her room to clean up before dinner and made a mental note to ask Tanak or Krey about this disappearing communication.

10

The unusual all-comm call came in the early afternoon and was heard only one time.

"Dr. Tanak and Officer Krey report to the bridge."

The rarity of an all-call signified its importance to both men, who went directly to the control room. Brightly lit monitors were discharging constantly updated information into the dimly lit room. Captain Lor was waiting for them when they entered and motioned them to a side station.

"We're just getting information in from home regarding light flares and weather systems which look like we could be heading into two pretty ominous super storms. Look at this data." Information began flowing across the counter where they were seated.

"We need to start making some decisions about timing our reentry to Cytar. It looks like we'll have a very narrow safe entry slot if we try to keep close to our original plan. If not, we need to stay out until it's feasible again. Tanak, tell me what you think in terms of Candidate health, and Krey, what are your feelings about the crews' morale in case we can't get in for a while. Also, we'll need to think about food supplies. We didn't count on long extended delays when we did the wake-ups."

Concerned expressions shown on both men while they studied the weather projections, which looked possibly life threatening.

"This is a dangerous confluence of systems. If weather weren't a factor, when were you planning on beginning the course back?" Krey was asking.

"Without the weather complication, the computers were saying within a week to ten days would be ideal. It could possibly be months longer if we miss this opening. Starting a few days early and trying to squeeze in between the systems might be our only feasible alternative. That's where we'd hope the weather data is accurate."

"What's the go/no go time frame for that decision?" Tanak wanted to know.

"We have less than two days to watch for any changes in the forecast."

As they poured over data and ran projections of different scenarios, the anguished looks on the three faces told of the vital decision they were facing. Calculations and scenarios were analyzed and debated. As captain, the final decision and its consequences rested with Lor.

"According to this data, we can reach home in between the storms if we stay on course, but we would need to briefly increase propulsion. I trust the calculations and the ship, but this has never been done before. The other thing to keep in mind is that it would also mean that the shuttle would also need to travel at increased speed to stay ahead of the storm. Your thoughts?"

Tanak and Krey looked at each other. Tanak spoke first. "If you increase shuttle speed, it will require safety suits for all passengers, and we've never been able to update the older model suits we're using."

"I realize that, but they've been checked and passed inspections. The use of the suits was already included into the projection. We have more than enough for all on board."

The air was heavy with concern. The crew's and passengers' lives depended on a correct decision. Additionally, the loss of this transport could ultimately cost the failure of their communities.

Lor finally said, "Okay, I'll give it 24 hours, then we'll meet again to see if anything changes in the forecasts. Then I need to make a decision. In the meantime, give me your thoughts on the crew and passengers."

When they met again the following day, Lor said, "The weather data remains steady. The projected computer analysis shows high confidence in the prediction of when the light flares will reach the planet's atmosphere and create some chaos, which is not for one week. They're saying the worst ground storm will occur two days before that. If we can miss that and get in during this narrow time frame, we could get everyone safely home before the trailing storm, which also looks very significant."

Krey's eyes widened. "That doesn't give us much margin of error if we go early. Do you think you can get us in during that narrow critical time slot?"

"I don't think I'd consider it if I didn't have confidence in this transport's speed and reliability. But it looks like we'd need to start course in three days. We can't risk any disruptions in our guidance systems from any strange electromagnetic activity if we get caught outside of this specific time frame."

Tanak and Krey were quiet for a moment before Tanak said, "In terms of the Candidates' physical and mental health, I'm sure they can handle the trip in. It's not that far from the original plan."

Krey added, "The morale of the crew would definitely be better if we landed sooner, but every one of them will be fine if you decide to extend."

"Then, I'm going to release the weather data and the choices we are facing and give them the chance to give input into the decision." Lor said in a definitive tone.

Within an hour, the information went out on all of the crew's readers and wrist coms. They had 12 hours to respond before the captain would make a decision.

11

The announcement for the meeting time was delivered to the crew's wrist comms and readers. Everyone eagerly waited to hear the captain's decision regarding the trip home, and the transport's final checkout information was immensely important. This meant the long voyage was coming to a conclusion, and no one wanted to be held up at the last minute for not completing their reports, checking in any outstanding equipment or cleaning their quarters. The thirty-three crew in attendance filed into a conference area, talking as they were seated. They were surprised and quieted quickly when Captain Lor joined Tanak and Krey at the head table with the 2nd officer who usually went over basic end-of-tour protocol.

Lor looked out at the group, all sitting in their working uniforms of dark pants and blue shirts, and got right to the point.

"As you know, we're in a bit of a precarious situation, but based on your feedback and our current data, we are not waiting. We have just begun to set the coordinates for our ship's course back home in an effort to miss the first storm and land before the trailing super storm." The crew began clapping, smiling and shaking their heads in affirmation.

"There's more," he continued, as the crew quieted. "I'm sure you've all heard rumors and read the announcements of the union bonding ceremony and have had time to consider if this is something you are interested in. If there is sufficient interest, we will bond a total of 10 couples on this trip. Five men and five women may be chosen from our group of Candidates."

Crew members were looking and nodding at each other and low murmurs could be heard.

"Please consider carefully before you make a decision like this. These ceremonies are meant to pledge you both for life, and as you know, this can be difficult for travelers like us. Think carefully, and if you are positive that you are ready, and you believe the Candidates you are considering are ready to adapt to their new life, have your applications completed and submitted for review within the next two days. The ceremony will take place in four days, and, if all goes well, we will dock shortly after. Are there any questions?"

A woman stood and asked, "Are all the Candidates eligible?"

Tanak answered, "Yes, the entire pool is eligible on this trip."

More murmuring. A man in the back stood.

"What happens if two of us choose the same Candidate?"

Krey spoke, "That rarely happens, but if so, both applications will be reviewed, and the data will determine with whom the Candidate is deemed most compatible. Our selection algorithms are very good and have an excellent record of finding the best matches for success. However, if there is an issue, we will make sure that the crew member's and the Candidate's backgrounds are double checked. Also, keep in mind that crew rank can also be a deciding factor."

He paused for emphasis before he added, "Our decisions are final."

Lor stood, "I will turn this meeting over to Officer Crelyn, who will go over your final transport checkout details. Final instructions for the bonding ceremony will be delivered to your readers."

Tanak and Krey followed him out of the room while Crelyn began speaking.

Krey had trouble sleeping that night, thinking of how near they were to end of their expedition and the new issues facing them. The weather and flare situations were bad enough, and now this bonding news was on his mind. Bonding ceremonies during travel were not that common. The only woman he had been interested in a while was Mara, but with his job, he wasn't sure if he should be thinking of a permanent relationship. Life on long journey voyages was difficult both physically and mentally. He was in his wheelhouse with his work, always self-assured, competent, and hardworking; but in a personal relationship, his confidence waned. He sometimes felt as if he were venturing out into no-man's land without life support; but his keen interest in her did seem different, more natural, more comfortable, and definitely more intriguing.

He was undeniably attracted to her and continually enjoyed being with her. She always seemed so happy to see him, and he appreciated her interest in the new things she learned during their visits. He tried to sleep, but thoughts of Mara kept resurfacing, rolling around, building strength. He wished Lor hadn't decided on this ceremony. What if she moved to another settlement, and he never saw her again, or worse, he watched her vowed to someone else? That thought bothered him. Should he wait and see what happens when they're home, or should he decide now? This life decision plagued him, knowing it would affect both of their futures forever. He finally lapsed into a fitful sleep and woke in a dour mood.

12

Two mornings later, the announcement appeared on all of the Candidates' readers when they awoke. There was to be a bonding ceremony at 1400 hours the following day. Candidates would be notified if they have been chosen to attend the ceremony and, if so, would be escorted to the event by their Helper. Mara had no idea what this meant and anxiously went to breakfast. The room was in high agitation. Several came to ask Mara about the notice on the reader.

"I'm sorry, I don't know anything. I've never heard of such a thing," was all she could say.

She needed to find Krey, or maybe Cali could tell her something. On her way to her work assignment, she saw Cali in the hallway. "Cali, what is this bonding event?"

The response came with the usual tepid smile, "I'm sorry, I can't respond to that now."

"Where is Krey? I need to talk to him." Mara's voice had a distressed tone.

Cali's unemotional reply was delivered with her frozen smile. "I will let him know that you wish to speak with him."

She turned in her methodical way and walked down the hall, leaving Mara looking after her and shaking her head in frustration. She had difficulty concentrating at work with her thoughts always wondering about what this bonding ceremony meant. After work, she paced the halls where everyone seemed to be in a rush, hoping to see Tanak or Krey. She was on her way to the dining area when Krey came around the corner, walking with another crew member. When he saw Mara, he said something to the woman, who continued on, and he walked up to her with a warm hello.

"Krey, what does this bonding ceremony mean?" Her face was unusually serious, and her normal smile was missing.

He spoke quietly, "Captain Lor is allowing the crew members to apply for a life commitment ceremony. Up to five men and five women Candidates may be chosen.

"Life commitment? What does that mean?" Her voice was strained.

He continued, trying to keep the explanation short and undetailed.

"Crew members may choose someone they wish to be with at home. Applications are carefully screened for the best potential for success. The top paired applicants and their Candidates may go through a ceremony in which they basically pledge their lives to each other."

Why is this familiar? Her anxious mind was unable to process an explanation, so she quickly dropped the thought and moved on.

"Does the Candidate have any say in this?"

"Usually not," he said gently. "But the criteria for selection are so good that Candidates usually are very happy with the choices."

She started to ask another question when he interrupted.

"I have to go now. Don't worry. We'll be docking in just a day or so." He turned and continued quickly down the hall, leaving Mara very feeling very unsettled.

At dinner she told Genna and Omi the little she had learned, and they quickly disseminated the information to the rest of the women. Reactions varied from anxiety and excitement to hope. The room seemed to clear out sooner than normal, as each woman left to deal with their own thoughts. Mara went to the more occupied than usual Meditation, and sat, trying, without success to clear her brain, which only flooded with more questions. *Where are we docking, and where will I go? Where is home?* She decided that the bonding ceremony would be of little consequence to her, but she wondered who would be chosen for this unpredicted event. The serenity of the room eventually began to calm her, but she returned to her room with nebulous concerns still wandering through her mind.

13

The next morning, Mara was lying in bed, awake after a disturbed night of sleep, when there was a soft tap on the door, and Cali entered carrying a garment bag.

"Good morning," she said as the room window brightened. "You have been chosen to participate in the ceremony today. This is the clothing that you will wear to our special rite. I will come and escort you after your breakfast. You should be honored," she added as she left with her usual smile.

Mara's heart quickened and her thoughts spun. She didn't know anyone enough to be with for life. The men she had worked with were all good people, but she had no really deep feelings toward them. The only men she was genuinely fond of were Tanak and especially Krey, and she knew they wouldn't be interested in Candidates. Somehow, she would have to decline.

Breakfast was anything but normal, with the loquacious women trying to determine if anyone in their group would be in the Ceremony. It didn't take long for them to learn that Omi and Mara would participate, and they speculated about men and women from the other groups. Omi seemed as apprehensive as Mara about what their future would hold. Mara was trying to think about what they could do, when a thought unexpectedly crossed her mind.

"Omi," she asked suddenly, "where did you come from before this ship?"

Omi stared blankly.

"I guess I don't remember right now. My mind is so occupied with what's happening today."

They were interrupted by Omi's Helper, Reeva. "Please follow me for a special morning."

As they left the room, several girls offered a restrained "good luck." They were taken to a room with low lights and soft music.

"This is our spa room," Reeva explained with a smile similar to Cali's. "A delicious drink is prepared for you."

A steaming, dark drink was presented, which produced aromas of berries and mocha chocolate. It was in the same lightweight, yet sturdy, gray vessel which was now common to them. The drink was delectably soothing and had an immediate relaxing effect on them. Reeva ushered them back to where three other women from other groups were waiting. The morning passed with the calming indulgences of a facial, a massage, and having nails shaped and buffed to a shine. They could not tell whether it was the massage or the drink, but they became very tranquil as their hair was styled for them. After a light lunch was served, Helpers brought in the garments.

Each was given an ankle length dress they had never before seen. The material was a soft very light blue, with a hint of palest green when the fabric moved. It felt velvety smooth against the skin as Mara put it on. She was led to her full-length reflection, a first she'd seen since she began this journey. She stared at herself. The long dress was beautiful, flaring slightly near the bottom. The elbow-length sleeves were lacy except for the solid fabric lightning shape running down the middle of each arm. Below the inch-high collar which encircled the neck were three diamond shaped cutouts. She turned and saw a wide translucent hood on the back. Reeva came up and gave her silver-toned strapped sandals. She returned to the spa room where the other four women were assembling. *So beautiful.* They were all in similar dress, with only slight variations, and all wore silver sandals.

"It is time," Reeva said.

14

Cali and three other Helpers had now joined the group. Each Helper arranged their Candidate's hood on their head. The hood was shear and wide enough to create a slight cape over the shoulders. Cali walked with Mara as they proceeded to a gathering room. Her thoughts were foggy, strangely calm mixed with a suppressed nervousness. They stood together behind a clear screen where five men from other groups had been waiting. They, too, were dressed in new clothing of identical dark blue, fitted pants and a tailored shirt. Other crew members were coming in and taking seats in the open area, talking quietly.

A side door opened and Captain Lor, Tanak, Krey and two women entered with purposeful strides and took seats at the front table. They were all dressed in formal looking uniforms, deep navy-blue pants, with a light blue turtleneck collared shirt, and a buttoned jacket. A lightning emblem could be seen on the collar. The room became quiet, and Lor let the silence settle on the audience before he began.

"Welcome to the last day of a very successful mission. This was possible because of your hard work and careful diligence on a precarious voyage. Our home communities are extremely grateful for all of your efforts. Our crew and Candidates have traveled and adjusted well, which makes our life bonding ceremony a fitting conclusion to our journey. However, as you know, we have been informed of upcoming turbulent weather conditions at home, so," he paused here for emphasis, "as per your wishes, we will continue with the bonding ceremony, albeit a much shortened one. I understand why no one wants to bypass the entry now and risk another few weeks or months out until we can find a new safe vector into port. So, our ship continues at speed to a viable home course in order to get you all to shelter before the next dangerous weather arrives. I assume that your presence here means that you are all cleared, packed and ready to depart at a moment's notice if need be."

He waited briefly as he scanned the room.

"At this time, Vicar Kneara will begin our Ceremony."

Kneara rose and proceeded to a center circle. Around her shoulders lay a long, light blue vestment with a lightning symbol on each end of the stole.

"Ladies and gentlemen, we give thanks for our safe passage through this dangerous expedition. We give thanks for our exceptional crew and Candidates as we begin our ceremony. The selected Candidates may now join us."

The Helpers walked next to the Candidates as they entered the main area and lined up creating an aisle way, with the five men on one side and the five women facing them. Once in place, the Helpers stood behind their Candidate. Omi grabbed Mara's hand and squeezed it. The lighting on the audience dimmed, leaving the Candidates on display.

Mara's mind was going numb. The first female crew member was announced with the Candidate she chose. Mara had met Kep, a bright affable man who had often worked with this crew member.   She heard speaking and the couple's response without really being able to concentrate on what was said.

A male crew member was then called up, and Omi smiled and looked relieved when her name was announced. Mara remembered Lan and knew, from Omi's numerous conversations, that they would be happy together. They stood before the vicar with words spoken and something was attached to Omi's wrist before more words were spoken. It was all happening so quickly.

Mara stared at the wall straight ahead.   Her face was unchanged, but her heart was pounding, and her eyes widened when she saw Draven walk up to the vicar.   Then, as if through a deep ocean of cloudy, turbulent water, she heard her name called.

Her feet refused to move. She stared straight ahead, seeing nothing.   Her name was called again followed by a movement somewhere near the front table.   People in the audience began looking at each other with questioning glances.   Moments seemed to drag on forever in Mara's anxious mind, before Lor's voice could be heard.

"Ladies and gentlemen, we have an unusual circumstance which needs a brief discussion."   Mara began looking for a way to escape the room, her mind reeling.

There were quiet whispers among the observers until, at last, Lor spoke. "One of our senior officers has filed a claim to substitute.   As you know, this is very unusual, but allowed in our regulations, so we ran the request through our program, and it shows an excellent match. Therefore, the substitution will be permitted at this time."

Comments of surprise rippled through the crew members. Before Mara could move, Krey walked up, took her hand and led her before the vicar. The vicar raised her eyebrows and smiled at Krey before she began.

"With this service, we pledge Krey and Mara to a life together, caring for one another, understanding and supporting each other. Krey, as the one who has chosen, do you agree and vow to accept this bonding?" Krey turned and looked straight into Mara's eyes.

"Yes, I wholeheartedly agree and accept," he answered clearly.

"Mara, as the chosen one, do you agree and vow to accept this bonding?"

She couldn't speak. Krey's eyes were boring into hers, almost pleading. At last, she managed a quiet, mere whisper of a "yes."

"Let it be entered on record that the chosen replied yes," the vicar confirmed. "Present your arms, please."

Krey took Mara's hand and lifted it toward the vicar. For the first time, she noticed another woman standing near the vicar, handing her what looked like two identical bracelets. One was placed on Krey's left wrist and one on Mara's right. As soon as it was clasped on her wrist, it was immediately drawn and attached to Krey's bracelet. She stared at a blinking white light which glowed from beneath each of them. They were quite beautiful she decided, made from the same ubiquitous gray, metallic material with which she was so familiar. They each had intricately inscribed symbols of an infinity line with a lightning bolt intersecting the infinity crossover line. The light was radiating heat and was changing to an orange color and blinking faster and warmer.

Vicar Kneara spoke, "As the stars are seen into the vastness of infinity, may these symbols always remind you of your pledge to honor one another forever."

Mara barely heard the words. Her bracelet was beginning to feel uncomfortably warm, and she looked questioningly at Krey. He was still gazing at her with an assuring smile and held her hand still. The light quickly changed to red and, just as her skin began to feel unbearably hot and burning, the light glowed solid red and the bracelets released.

They were removed as the vicar smiled and said, "You are officially bonded on the transport *Superstes*. Congratulations Krey and Mara."

As they walked out of the room, Mara caught sight of Draven watching them with eyes like slits and lips drawn into a tight line.

15

Her burning wrist demanded attention, and she saw raised red welts forming which were identical to the pattern on the bracelet.

She was about to speak when Cali appeared, and Krey immediately spoke to her.

"Please prepare her for departure. I need to get back right away."

He hugged Mara. "It's going to be all right," he whispered to her before he hurried away.

Cali led the way back to her room, where she placed a cool strip of thick cloth which immediately curved around Mara's wrist. Cali gave her a one-piece outfit made of thicker pliable material.

"You will change now into your regular clothes and put this suit over your clothes." Mara slipped the dress off quickly and handed it to Cali.

As she was leaving Cali said, "I will return this garment, and you will pack all of your belongings. You will not be returning to this room. I will come soon to take you to our departure area."

Mara's mind was spinning from too many new and unexpected events in the emotionally confusing day. She still did not feel like herself, and try as she might to calm down, the day was still in a cluttered confusion, where too much happened too quickly for her brain to fully comprehend. She dressed and packed with a sense of urgency and managed to get into the outfit, closing it up to the stiff circular collar. The suit's material had a very unique texture, slightly thicker than her normal clothing but surprisingly supple, feeling very strong, yet smooth and soft. The legs and arms, too long for her, wrinkled at the ends.

She slung her bag over her shoulder and was ready when Cali held the door open for her to follow. There were others in the halls now, all in similar suits and heading in the same direction into a section of the ship the Candidates had never seen. *This ship must be huge, much bigger than I imagined.* They turned, entered what seemed like a massive chamber to someone so accustomed to small spaces. When all the Candidates were accounted for, a Helper pressed markings on the wall, and the thick door behind them closed and locked.

The chamber had rows of seats, each with some kind of head covering attached and draped across the back. Candidates were stashing bags and being seated in fitted padded chairs which had a soft molded partition between the calves of the legs. Cali led Mara past the rows of seats in the middle section where the others were settling in. She locked eyes with Genna for a moment before Cali pointed to her seat along the wall. As soon as she sat down, the leg sides of the chair from the knees down raised and gently pressed against the lower half of her legs. Almost in panic, she looked around and was somewhat reassured to see the same had happened to everyone.

A voice announced, "As a safety precaution, please attach the hood to your suit."

She watched Helpers assist others as they claimed the coverings from the back of their seats. She struggled to put hers over her head, trying to turn it for a better fit, when a Helper arrived to assist with its placement. As soon as it was aligned for proper vision with the clear shield, the hood-type apparatus became rigid. She momentarily became claustrophobic before realizing she could breathe normally. Cali seated three others and checked several rows before she came and adjusted Mara's sleeves and pant legs, making sure they fit snuggly and closed completely over the hands and feet. A momentary unsettling feeling of entombment was experienced with the covered hands, feet and head, but she found comfort from watching Cali nearby. After a final inspection, her Helper took a narrow seat next to her.

When all five Helpers were at last seated, flat, curved safety restraints lowered from the wall and held their shoulders in place. Mara heard two clicking sounds, looked over and saw Cali's head resting back into an indented headrest attached to the wall. Her eyes had closed, and she was inactive. Mara scanned the room to find that the four other AI Helpers also seemed to be asleep, and all of the other passengers had the same safety bar restraints extend from the backs of their seats. Again, she and Genna locked eyes for a moment, as if gathering reassurance from each other.

A voice next to Mara's head began speaking. "Stay seated for the remainder of our high-speed journey. We will be entering home port atmosphere soon." Mara shuddered. *What atmosphere, and where do they think I'd be going in this contraption?* Ship, ship, she always wanted to think of a ship on an ocean, but her mind could never really follow the reasoning. Where were they going now? To one of the undersea habitats? To one of the space habitats? Now, all of the tangled incongruities in her experiences were rolling around in her head and disappearing before she could find any solutions. Her stressful exhaustion was forcing thoughts and questions into oblivion.

A slight vibration began in her seat, and she soon began to feel light headed before the supplemental oxygen in her face shield adjusted appropriately. The covering on her legs began to apply more pressure, and she was starting to perspire under the extra layer of suit. She looked over to Cali for reassurance, but she remained immobile with closed eyes. The faces of the other Candidates were devoid of emotion, some just staring, while others seemed asleep. Gradually, more pressure pushed against her entire body. A nauseous wave rippled through her body causing a fatigue to wash over her. Musical tones became audible, at first barely perceptible, before increasing to a soft level. The ancient tones from the Solfeggio scale were set at frequencies meant to calm the mind, and she drowsily watched fellow passengers until her eyes closed.

16

A distant voice, then a shaking and pushing against the shoulder gave the muddled, fitful, off-and-on sleeper the wake-up. Cali was pulling on Mara's hand and handing her the shoulder bag with the other.

"We have arrived. Remove your outer suit. It is time to go. I will escort you."

The shoulder restraints had retracted and her legs were free. Cali assisted with her sleeves and pant legs, allowing Mara to pull off her head shield which lost its rigidity when detached. She looked around while she unfastened and peeled off the one piece covering and threw it on her seat. Everyone was getting ready to leave the chamber following Cali, while the other Helpers were already staying behind to collect the discarded suits.

The travelers were walking on a slanted floor, descending to a lower level before entering a narrow walkway. The pace slowed to a mere shuffle when they converged into a single file line, then waited to be scanned with thin bands of colored light emitted from the ceiling and walls. They emerged into a larger room where several other Candidates were standing and watching crew members for direction. Mara, unable to find Krey, joined Omi and Genna to wait.

"They say we're leaving. I wonder if we'll see each other again," Genna said as they were being formed into four lines which corresponded to four large doors. "Do you know where we're going?"

Mara, with unsteady legs, only managed to say "I have no idea," as she scanned the room.

The air here had a different smell, but she did not know how to describe the change. Inhaling deep breaths, she confirmed a definite difference. *Maybe this is what unfiltered air smells like, odorless, almost undetectably different, yet somehow fresher.*

More Candidates were entering the area, some with their newly bonded partners. In front of each of the four wide exit doors, vehicles were lined up, ready to transport passengers to their destinations before the weather deteriorated. Helpers assisted in keeping travelers moving quickly and adeptly to the outside where several people shared each transport.

The atmosphere in the room was charged with the relief, the excitement, the impatience, and the anticipation of returning home after a long absence. Energy exuded from the lines like the pent-up drive of high-speed shuttle pilots waiting for take-off. The crew members were continually monitoring their wrist comms for information on their departure vehicles and weather conditions. Names of Candidates were beginning to be announced, and they were efficiently led out of the building.

Hoping to find Krey, Mara's eyes continued to roam the room, searching the crew member's blue shirts through the mass of black and greens. Steadily, people continued to leave in small groups while others watched and waited. Lan arrived for Omi and said it was time to leave for home. She and Genna each gave Mara a hug and then, the three walked out a door which quickly closed after them, leaving Mara feeling abandoned and wondering where home was.

The large area, which minutes before oozed the energy of hyperactivity, was now a hollow, echoing space. Still no sign of Krey, but dependable Cali was carrying a coat and walking toward Mara.

"It is getting late. You will need this now." She held up a long, dark burgundy coat with a wide, thick, fur collar. Mara put it on, feeling its softness envelop and comfort her.

"Dr. Tanak and Officer Krey are on their way," Cali continued. "Your home ground transport is waiting. It has been a pleasure to work with you on this trip. I wish you well."

It was almost too much for Mara when she realized Cali must be saying a final goodbye.

"Thank you, Cali, for all of your help," and then, she couldn't resist the urge to hug her. When she was released, Cali tilted her head, blinked several times and gave to Mara what seemed to be her kindest smile, then turned and walked away.

Mara, with a strange light headedness, was feeling deserted, standing alone watching Cali leave, and fighting back tears. Hearing her name called, she turned and was relieved to see Krey and Tanak, both wearing long, dark gray coats, striding toward her. They carried cases strapped across their shoulders, and each had a large bag independently rolling after them. She walked quickly toward them, and Krey immediately took her hand and led her to the exit door.

"Our home transports are waiting," he said with a despondent urgency in his voice. "Tanak, we'll talk soon."

"Yes, and safe travel to you both," he hesitated and added, "and, again, my sincere condolences." He shook Krey's hand and hurried out ahead of them.

Mara was unprepared for the brutal cold which instantly pierced the skin. She clutched the coat tightly and pulled the collar up around her face. The sky was darkening as a nearly white orb was swiftly sinking on the horizon.

Tanak's vehicle was already pulling away as theirs pulled up and stopped before them. It was a strange looking ground transport, with the front and back having the same aerodynamic slope from the cab, making it difficult to determine which direction it would travel. Krey opened the door, took her arm and guided her into a seat before grabbing his bag and jumping in beside her.

They were alone, but a male voice spoke, "Welcome back, Officer Krey."

Krey answered quickly, "Thank you; are all of our belongings on board?"

"Yes,sir. Are we ready?"

He responded immediately, "Yes, and activate fast mode."

The weather system made for a dicey landing, and he was glad to be back on solid ground. It was such an unusual homecoming without the normal welcoming attention, the festive and congratulatory groups to greet them. There would have been a speech or two and video coverages disseminated to all households, but he guessed the weather system would have interfered with any attempt at clear transmissions. Once on the ground, there was no time to linger; everyone knew to be very respectful of the storms here. This was no time to be out, and he didn't mind the quiet return. The sooner he could be home the better.

Mara was set back in her seat by the quick take off. She looked out of the window, sensing an elevated perspective, but it was difficult to determine in the rapidly fading light. At one point, she thought she detected some strangely shaped buildings, but through the near darkness she could only detect a few lights and wondered if the speed of their travel was distorting her vision. High in the murky sky, she could see ominous flashes of massive lightning. She became aware that Krey had put his arm around her, and it suddenly felt good to be out of the cold and next to him.

17

It was difficult to judge speed and distance in the darkness, but she did not think they had traveled very long before the vehicle slowed and entered a downward sloping drive and stopped between a low lighted building and an elevated bank.

Krey opened the door and helped Mara out before leaning back in to put his bag on the ground and said, "Remain here until luggage is unloaded before you dock."

Cold shivers spiraled through Mara when the wind suddenly swirled around and blew her collar up against her cheek. He led her down to a door, which opened before they could reach it. A kind looking woman greeted them, hugging Krey with a big smile and ushering them quickly inside.

"Oh, welcome, welcome home! Come in, come in. We've been worried about your return with the coming storm. We're so happy to have you back safely; you've been so missed. And we were happy to hear your news!" Without a pause she turned, "You must be Mara. You must be a special young woman to capture this guy!" She grabbed Mara's hand and steered her further inside.

"Bertie, Bertie, they're here!" A tall, affable looking man approached with a wide smile.

"Hello, hello!" he called, taking Krey's hand and shaking it with energy, his other hand resting on Krey's shoulder.

"So good to have you back! Everyone's been monitoring your inbound progress, and we've all breathed a sigh of relief now that you've safely arrived." He kept holding the handshake, looked into Krey's eyes and asked, "You've heard the news, then?"

"Yes, it was reported just before we boarded our shuttle. I suspected as much when there was never any information or updates. It's the specter we always have to be prepared for here." And then, as if there was something too painful to dwell on, he immediately changed his solemn expression with a tenuous smile.

"Can't tell you how good it is to be back," he said, drawing Bertie into an embrace with his other arm. He then turned for introductions and said, "This is Mara, and these are two very important people in my life, Gracelyn and Robert."

Pleasant comments were exchanged before Gracelyn announced that she had a hot soup dinner all prepared for them.

"You can show Mara to your room, while I put a light dinner on for my weary travelers. Does Bertie need to get anything from your ground transport?"

"Mara's bag hasn't been linked yet, so that should be it." She no longer had any recollection of bringing her bag in from the ship. His travel bag was sitting on the floor directly behind him. She watched Bertie pick it up and place it near the wall. Their coats were deposited in a closet before Krey grabbed his bag and led her down a short hall to a room on the left.

"This will be your room for as long as you wish," he explained. "Our bedroom is right next door at the end of the hall, but I know it will take time for you to feel comfortable there. You can freshen up here across the hall." He squeezed her hand before adding, "I'll knock for you in a few minutes, and we'll go have some dinner with Gracelyn and Bertie."

Mara looked around at the small, but cheerful room, a stark contrast to what she had been accustomed on the *Superstes*. The full-sized bed, decorated with a bright yellow and white cover, had barely enough room for a narrow walkway on both sides. Two inset wall lights, one on either side of the bed, and a petite, yet pleasingly proportioned, chair seemed crammed in the corner to complete the room. There was a closet, and across the hall was the door which led to a bathroom. Bathroom, she hadn't thought of that word in a long time.

This room was also refreshingly different from her streamlined "personal room". It was not big, but seemed palatial in comparison to her previous accommodations. Long tiles shimmered in the light, and a full-sized towel was hanging on a cylindrical bar. She ran her fingers along the smooth bar, which caught her attention. It was not the gray metal she with which she was familiar, but composed of a unique, almost concrete looking material.

She washed her hands with fragrant, herbal scented soap and was drying them, when she noticed the cloth cover Cali had put on her wrist, and realized her skin was no longer burning. She began to peel off the bandage, which unveiled a dark, smooth image of an infinity symbol with a lightning bolt clearly marked on her skin. A closer inspection revealed a miniature, perfectly scrolled K in one side of the infinity loop and an ornate M in the other. She rubbed her wrist, now completely smooth with no pain. Krey's knock on the door interrupted her thoughts, and he led her in for dinner.

Heavenly aromas filled the air as they entered a warm, compact room with a table and four chairs near the center and a sleek cooking area along one wall. Mara made a quick survey of the counter with a sink under a digital image of a fruit bowl, a cabinet hugging each edge of the picture, and a familiar built-in all-cook appliance. On the opposite wall, facing the backyard, stood the only other furniture, a narrow open-shelved cabinet sitting by a wide clear door.

"Soup's on," Gracelyn announced. "Come and sit."

The table was already set, and she began ladling into bowls and set the first one in front of Mara. The rich aroma of chicken and vegetables caused her mouth to water, igniting her appetite. She could not remember when she had last eaten, and she was almost overcome with the intoxicating smells of the food. While three more bowls were filled, she stared into her rich soup, transfixed by the fresh orange carrot pieces bobbing as if to tease her, the crescent shaped celery slices, and, wonder of wonders, the beautiful chunks of chicken. She recalled the food she was accustomed to eating, the food with the tiny, often rehydrated vegetables and mystery proteins.

Bertie brought her back to the present when he placed a basket of crusty bread between her and Krey. He said a short blessing followed by "dig in!"

Mara needed no coaxing. Suddenly acknowledging her thirst, she first drank water from the container at her place. She could hardly pay attention to the conversation as she turned her attention to the beautiful food before her. Forcing herself to eat slowly, carefully, she prolonged the enjoyment of each mouthful of the tender, richly seasoned chicken pieces, carrots, rice and savory broth. The piquancy of the rich flavors danced in her mouth. This was real food, so different from her diet of the past many weeks.

"This is so delicious," she managed to say between mouthfuls.

"Thank you." Gracelyn smiled, clearly pleased by the compliment. "Well, I decided to fix some real food in celebration of Krey's homecoming. The prepared meals didn't seem appropriate."

"It's very much appreciated, Gracelyn," Krey said, already helping himself to another bowl. She heard Gracelyn and Bertie talk about the house and local town news, but her mind was on her food, and her body was tiring. Their conversation was occasionally interrupted by bright flashes of lightning and winds which were increasing in velocity. A booming thunder clap startled Mara.

"Here comes that storm." Bertie said. "You were lucky to get in when you did. Supposed to be a mammoth electrical event later tonight." As if to accentuate his remarks, a piercing blast seemed to penetrate the entire house. "I think it's time for the shutters."

A quiet humming motor sound was heard, and the dinner and conversations continued normally. When Mara had finished eating, she noticed Krey looking at her with a kind smile.

"I'll help you clean up in a minute, Gracelyn, but I think Mara needs to rest now."

In her best mock stern voice Gracelyn answered, "I won't have it! Not on your first night back! You can help Bertie with your belongings. This won't take a minute, and then Bertie and I are off to our house. I'll check back in the morning to help with breakfast and more catching up." She was collecting their dishes and was pleased to see that not one grain of rice or a crumb of bread remained.

Mara stood. "Thank you for the delicious dinner."

"You're welcome, dear. You've had a long journey. Have a good rest and you'll feel like a new person in the morning. I've put a little dress for you in the guest closet in case you'd like something fresh to wear in the morning."

Krey grabbed her bag from the front entry where Bertie had deposited it and led her to the bedroom. "Remember, I'm right next door if you need anything."

He lingered, standing close to her, wanting to tell her how happy he was that she was here and how much the life ceremony meant to him, but the words wouldn't form. In the end he just hugged her and left the room.

18

Mara was awakened by a thunderous crash. An explosion was the first thought entering her jumbled brain, near frozen with fear. The room emitted no light, and she could not remember where she was. She was disoriented, trying desperately to remember, but her mind was dark and blank. There was a second crack more ferocious than the first, so sudden that a short cry escaped before she could control it. Her door opened and a faint light crept in as Krey entered and sat on the bed. She was trembling and cold.

He held her closely, saying, "It's okay, everything is okay. This is the electrical storm we were anticipating and the reason we needed to dock so quickly. Everyone got home safely." Another violent boom made her body shudder. If only her mind would clear. She heard Krey talking again.

"The exterior shutters activated, so the house is secure. This should be over by morning. The auxiliary power is on now, and I'll sit here until you feel better."

She detected a weak light coming from somewhere near the floor as she rested her head against him. Gradually the day's unusual events began bobbing to the surface of her murky brain. Her body slowly began to relax in his arms, his warmth reassuring. When she was ready to lie down, she pulled the covers up tightly, curled her knees up and blinked away the tears of total exhaustion. The angry winds persisted, but the earlier deafening thunderous sounds were not repeated.   She did not know how long Krey sat by her, only that she was alone when she woke up.

Judging from how refreshed her mind and body felt in the morning, she sensed she had several hours of good sleep. The first thing she did was walk to her window and attempt to push up a thick shade to take in the view. At her first touch, the shade rose automatically, and she then realized that the shade was between layers of a clear window material. She happily looked through a real window with a view. It was at ground level, but still allowed her to see a countryside scattered with a few small dwellings squatting with lopsided sloping roofs and walls that had oddly curved edges. Such strange little houses with no sharp corners on any building. Bright crystal-clear atmospheric light washed over the buildings and scarce, low growing plants. The cloudless sky belied the previous night's frightening storm.

When she looked out into the hall, she saw that Krey's bedroom door was open and the room seemed unoccupied. She turned back, opened the closet door and looked in at a large empty space, save for the dress Gracelyn had mentioned the previous night. The casual, coral-colored dress was hanging like a shrine of new brightness, waiting to be adored. Mara gazed at it lovingly, held it, touched its soft fabric to her cheek, pleased with its freshness after the monotony of wearing the same green and black clothing for so many repetitive days. She marveled at her uplifted spirits, a combination, she presumed, of sleep, the simple pleasures of an outdoor view, and a new colorful dress.

The house was quiet when she took a short but luxurious shower by ship standards. Gracelyn was right, she decided; she did feel like a new person as she dressed in the new outfit. She unpacked her bag and hung up the shirts, placed the folded pants and everything else on the wall of shelves opposite the hanging rod which was split between the upper shelf area and lower drawers. She was stretching to put the empty bag on the top shelf, when it startled her by moving down to within her reach. On closer inspection, she found that the shelves could rotate by a touch to any location on their circuit. Good to know, even though the small closet seemed oversized when compared to her need for storage. She ran her comber through her hair before going out to the dining area, where she was surprised to find Gracelyn at the table with a cup of tea, looking through a stack of magazines.

"Ah, good morning, Mara," she said brightly. "I see that dress fits you well. I tried to guess your size by what Krey communicated to me."

"Yes, it fits perfectly, thank you, and the color is so refreshing compared to what I've been used to. Now that I see this, I realize I was getting tired of wearing the same clothes every day; but at least they were comfortable, and I never had to decide what to wear."

"If you feel up to it, we can go later and pick up some more clothes for you. I don't imagine you'll want to keep wearing *Superstes* clothes all the time."

Without waiting for a reply, her words rolled on. "I hope you slept well through that storm. It was one of our bad ones. You were lucky to get in when you did. Woke me up, and I was grateful for the storm shutters. Bertie checked and all's well outside.   Oh, and look what Krey brought me from his expedition.

"They're old, but I don't care--real magazines! They're all but impossible to find anymore, collector items, they are. Everything is on our readers, but sometimes I just love to touch this paper and turn pages."

She was rubbing a hand along a smooth page, while passing a magazine across the table with the other.   Mara couldn't resist touching the periodical, so old and fragile feeling, with worn edges. While slowly turning pages, she realized that she never saw print on any paper on her journey. There was a moment of trying to recall, without success, the last time she saw text anywhere except in digital format. The magazines were curious, interesting to touch and look at, but strangely confining with no links. She watched Gracelyn flip back and forth between the pages and saw the interest in the articles.

She was staring at the pages when Gracelyn interrupted her thoughts.

"Listen to me going on. How about some breakfast?"

"Thank you, that sounds wonderful." It was easy to feel comfortable around Gracelyn.

"What's your pleasure: grains or eggs or cakes?"

Mara couldn't remember when she'd last eaten an egg. "An egg sounds perfect."

"Make yourself at home and I'll have it ready in no time," Gracelyn said as she was already heading to the counter.

Mara walked out into the room to her left, which was directly opposite the door they entered last night. It was a cozy sitting room, which she determined to be next to her bedroom. The ground level window revealed the same view onto the very naturally and sparsely, but somehow pleasantly, naturally landscaped backyard. The room was certainly not large, the size somehow reminding her of her previous quarters. In all the rooms she had seen, the walls were an unobtrusive neutral color, no doubt the unpainted tone of the building material. The small, modern, dark gray-toned sofa took up most of the depth of the room. A lighter gray chair was the only other furniture in the room, and both looked comfortable and in good condition. So sparse, just the basics, with the furniture sitting in close proximity in the small area.

Her eyes swept over the furniture again, and she realized that the construction framework for everything in this house used either the familiar gray metal or the new material she noticed in the bathroom. She was wondering about the lack of more wood use until she recalled the outdoor views with only ground-hugging plants. There simply would not be enough trees for building in this desert-like land. She turned back toward the entry door and decided to explore the rest of this little house later.

When she returned to the table, Gracelyn was bringing her food. The fried egg was framed by two pieces of hearty toasted bread, while three small fresh strawberries sat in a row, giving color to the plate. A cup of coffee was placed by her, and the aroma was rich and sumptuous. She held the cup and inhaled deeply. Gracelyn watched with a satisfied look.

"I've also got tea, but it looks like I guessed right with the coffee. Do you take milk flavor with it?"

"Yes, please," Mara answered before she even knew if that were true.

A watery, white liquid was offered and added to the coffee. She sipped and savored her hot drink before turning her attention to the beautiful dish before her. Gracelyn joined her with a slice of toast while Mara ate slowly, as if to prolong the enjoyment. She couldn't remember how long had it been since she had tasted a sweet, fresh strawberry, and found the tastes of each morsel of her meal intensely delicious.

"Have you seen Krey this morning?" she finally managed to ask between bites.

Gracelyn nodded, "He and Bertie went to town. Krey wanted to get something. Said they won't be long. I think he just wanted to see the town again and have a chance to visit with Bertie."

Mara was finishing her second cup of coffee when the men returned. *Krey looks so handsome.* This was the first time she'd seen him out of his ship's uniforms. He was wearing a solid-colored, dark brown, short- sleeve shirt, and she felt a strange sensation when she saw the matching infinity mark on his wrist. Krey gave her a smiling "good morning" while Gracelyn filled in the conversation with Bertie.

"Any luck in town?"

"Yeah, we had a nice visit catching up on things, and Krey found what he was looking for." Krey headed straight to the coffee carafe and poured himself a mug.

"Ah, the wonderful smell of fresh coffee! I don't know how you managed to get your hands on this, but it is fantastic. It's been a long time since we've had good coffee, or any coffee for that matter. We ran out of the powdered stuff on the trip about half way home."

Gracelyn was smiling with satisfaction, happy he was pleased.

"I put in an order for coffee almost a year ago with Kerry's Koffee. You're going to be surprised how he's grown that into a popular little business. Anyway, glad I was able to get it, and glad you're both enjoying it. There's a limited supply so you may as well enjoy it while you can."

As she took her dishes to the counter, Mara said, "Thank you for that perfect breakfast, Gracelyn, and the company."

"You're so welcome," she said, and then, turning to Bertie, she added, "I like that girl."

"Yeah, I do, too," Krey chuckled, coffee mug in hand, "Come on, Mara, I'll show you the yard."

He seemed much more relaxed and happier today without the stress and responsibilities on the ship.

19

A tray of curved, shaded eye bands sat on the small cabinet near the large, transparent door. Krey handed one to her and expanded his to cover his eyes, allowing the pliable material to adjust to his face.

"Our light is very intense today, so we'll need to protect our eyes," he said as they walked onto a patio and continued up a slope to a meandering path, which encircled a small section of the open ground between other houses. The barely discernable path was the only thing defining what could vaguely be called a yard.

Tired looking, meager, gray-green plants and a few small, drab flowers lay flattened and worn out from enduring the storm. Two miniature trees, trying not to be mistaken for shrubs, stood with thick trunks and a gnarly structure which, aside from some small broken branches, seemed no worse the wear from the night's severe weather. Mara did not recognize any of the plants, but the yard and the outdoor air were very refreshing. Her gaze reached beyond the yard to a low open path leading to a half sunken rectangular building, which she took for some sort of shelter.

"Is that a storage building?"

"That is the transport depot for this group of homes. It houses three identical personal transports to be shared by anyone who lives out here."

When she looked back toward the house, she saw that the middle of the house was divided by an enclosed walkway lined with a long window and a clear door. Krey followed her inquiring gaze.

"There are technically two homes here. Bertie and Gracelyn live in one side, and I have the other. However, since I've been gone so much, I told them they're welcome to use entire building if they'd like. I don't think they ever do, but when I'm home we often eat together, and I appreciate and really enjoy their company."

"They're very nice people. They make me feel so welcome," Mara said.

"They're the best. They make living here so much more pleasant, but now there's someone you should meet," Krey said as he walked to the side yard and opened a gate to a long, narrow fenced area with a shade structure.

"Stand behind me for a minute." A Chesapeake retriever came forward slowly, as if ready for battle, with his wavy, rusty brown hackles up and head low, sniffing the air.

"Rocket, it's me. Come here, come on, it's okay, come on," he coaxed in a calm voice. The dog walked slowly with his lip curled until recognition changed his demeanor. He bolted forward with tail spinning in frenetic exuberance when he discovered it was his long absent owner. Mara watched the happiness of dog and owner as they became reacquainted.

"This is Rocket," Krey managed to say while trying to pet and rough-house with the dog and keep him away from

Mara. Rocket was turning boisterous circles in his excitement. "He can be very unfriendly with new people, so I'm being a little cautious until he gets to know you."

The dog had other plans, coming right up to Mara with tail still wagging and a big panting dog smile. He was immediately rewarded with attention and affection while Krey stared, shaking his head.

"Well, he's making a liar out of me, but this is unusual. The few people he sees usually get a bark, a growl or barred teeth until he knows them, and he's very protective of Gracelyn, Bertie and me. He usually spends the night down in his kennel, but he often has the run of the place during the day, and I suspect he's often in Gracelyn and Bertie's house when I'm traveling. He's not as big as he should be because he wasn't able to get as much food as he needed when he was a puppy."

He seems huge to me. Mara was watching the joy in his unfettered energy as he bounded back and forth between them. Rocket eventually settled down and started exploring the yard as they walked back down toward the outdoor sitting area which was tucked under an overhang off the eating room. This small patio was created by the short, extended exterior sitting room wall and, she guessed, Gracelyn and Bertie's matching wall. She sat on a settee, and Krey, ignoring the nearby chair, sat next to her.

"I bought something for you this morning," he said as he set his coffee down and handed Mara a small package from his pocket.

She opened the soft bag and recognized a wrist comm, similar to the ones she had seen on the *Superstes*.

She was smiling when she looked up and said, "Thank you."

He held her wrist while placing the band, which immediately curled to fit as if custom made for her. It was thin and clear, save for three squares of color, each with a different symbol. She recognized a time symbol, and guessed at the others, maybe a message center, a calculator, or a calendar.

"It's all ready to use. Now we can talk to each other or Gracelyn or Bertie whenever we want. It will vibrate once if you get a call. Just briefly raise your fingers or make a slight fist to open or close a communication. You can talk normally, and you'll be heard."

For the moment, he decided to keep his instructions to the basics, but he did mention, as if in passing, "Later on, I'll show you how to use some of its many other capabilities, but for now, let's just use it for calling or for basic information." The implanted communication devices had been rejected in favor of these older wrist comms, and he wondered if she would remember using these before her voyage.

"When we were on the ship, I remember seeing you and Tanak project images on your hands from your wrist comms. You were doing something for your work, and I could see several icons appear on your hand, and they responded to your touch."

He was thinking how observant she was when he answered. "Yes, yours will do that, too, but for now, let's just practice the calling. We'll use only voice commands."

He called her wrist comm, and as they practiced, she observed this near stranger, with whom she had committed her life. She took in every detail of his face, his smile, his hands, and felt a growing kinship when her eyes rested on their identical bonding marks.

20

That afternoon, Gracelyn proceeded to show Mara how to call for the ground transport on her new wrist comm.

They were almost out the door when Mara turned and asked, "I forgot to ask Krey if this is self-charging, or do I need a charging block?"

Gracelyn looked puzzled for a moment before recognition shown on her face. She tightened her lips before a "don't you remember" slipped out.

"Oh, there's no worry. Yes, absolutely, it's self-charging. Your wrist comm converts your thermal energy into the current it needs, so you'll have continuous power wherever you are, plus the house is capable of continually charging any device within these walls."

She moved on to the task at hand. "Now, just so you know, we call our ground transports Gsports for short." Then barely contracting and relaxing her hand, she said, "Gsport, Gracelyn is ready for travel," demonstrating the simplicity of calling the vehicle to take them clothes shopping.

"Good afternoon, Gracelyn and Mara." The Gsport greeted them as they settled into the vehicle.

"Good afternoon. Main entrance, Gateway please," Gracelyn answered.

Mara was intrigued with the new vistas as they glided along. She could see a distant drone flying in their direction, a Gsport traveling far ahead of them and another which appeared to be returning empty to their home transport depot. The isolated housing area quickly changed to more desolate open land with a few grasses and low plants, but in the near distance she saw a distinctive settlement coming into view with half buried buildings, except for a middle section of three somewhat taller structures. As they came closer, she realized that all the buildings had the rounded edges and asymmetrical roof lines similar to Krey's home.

"Unusual rooflines, and the decorative metal on the peak edges is quite pretty," Mara commented.

"The non-symmetry helps withstand our tenacious wind storms, and the top metal structures, which curl over the peaks, contain spiral wind blades for power," Gracelyn explained. "Our wind storms are why none of the buildings are very tall. Most of them are like our house, built several feet into the ground and many have at least one-story underground. They build the long side of the roof angle facing windward in an attempt to alleviate storm damage. The use of the 3D industrial printers in our building construction has greatly strengthened these structures and helped them withstand our severe wind storms. What's really been helpful is that the actual constructing is surprisingly fast once they have the plans programmed and the material in place. Our structure took less than two days to build. That's why the buildings are identical in several places, making for more efficient construction."

Mara was inspecting the unique settlement of buildings as they drew closer. The vehicle eventually slowed and traveled to where the descending ground opened to a cavernous mouth of an entrance. The transport continued with decreased speed until it came in line with another vehicle dropping off passengers.

"You have arrived at the Gateway Complex," the now familiar male voice announced. The doors opened as the vehicle stopped. "Park," Gracelyn directed before leading Mara through a wide entry into an enclosed avenue of shops, offices, and business fronts.

With her eyes following upward to the light source, Mara saw a large, angled, opaque covering protecting the structure's interior walkways. The indoor community's walking paths meandered through a few scattered artificial plants in pretty planters and small water fountains with nicely placed seating areas. It reminded her of a bigger version of the special outdoor area on her ship. However, on closer inspection, this was also not as large as the first impression due to the artistic placement of objects within this interior space.

The compact area was immediately inviting, presenting a wonderful escape from the mono-toned outdoor vistas. A person passed them with a quick "hello Gracelyn" and a smile; another was exiting a door and crossing to other side of the open space. Two of the benches were occupied, one with a woman and child talking, another with a man viewing something on his reader which seemed to capture his total attention.

"We're going to a below-level store," Gracelyn was saying as she guided Mara toward elevators which brought them to an underground world totally unseen from the main entry. Gracelyn set off at a determined pace with Mara following behind, gaping at the narrow store fronts and short lanes which extended from the main artery.

They walked past brightly half-windowed doors with the digital business names scrolled above. One sign read Medical in strong reassuring letters; another had the word Sundries written in curly colorful letters. Across the way, a large lit sign announced The Crossing and underneath was an image of drink glasses and a knife and fork. Each business' display window exhibited an eye-pleasing graphic, some constant, some rotating and fading into new images. They passed a few more people coming and going with the purposeful strides of those who knew where they were going and why.

"I wasn't expecting all this," she remarked, walking quickly to keep up.

"Oh, sorry," Gracelyn said. "I didn't give you enough time to see the entrances to the apartments. Most of our residents live in this multiuse area, and it's over-built with the hope of future growth. Our housing development is quite rare. Krey's worked hard to achieve his higher-level role on transports, so he's earned and saved enough for the choice of a house with a little open space. I guess you could consider that a plus or a minus, depending on how tired you get of our climate and the monotonous views. You may have seen Captain Lor on our ship. He lives near an identical complex on the other side."

Mara wanted to ask questions, but they were approaching a store with a deep orange sign which uncreatively read Clothing. They entered a door with a quaint ornate handle which actually had to be pulled for the door to open. Quiet music added to the old-fashioned charm and an inviting ambiance greeted them. The room was narrow, deeper than wide, and initially presented shoppers with images of men's and women's clothing, but as Gracelyn walked toward the center, the images transformed into enticing images of only women's wear. A few actual clothing items were displayed, a pretty top with short sleeves, a long-sleeved shirt with a front closure, a pair of dark pants. A woman, with attractively styled hair and a perfectly fitted red dress, immediately turned her attention to them.

"Good afternoon and welcome. How may I assist you?" She projected a friendly yet professional tone.

Gracelyn answered, "This is Mara, Officer Krey's bond from the *Superstes*. We're here to select clothing from his suggestions, which he communicated earlier."

"Yes, of course, hello Mara. We have several lovely garments from which I'm sure you'll find satisfactory selections. Officer Krey has very good taste. Right this way, please."

They were led to a short hall where Mara was told to stand while a light beam took her measurements and saved them for future purchases. Outfits were then brought out with styles utilitarian rather than high fashion, with classic lines, a few basic colors and subtle changes in cut and line for variety. Mara tried on several outfits in a private dressing area, and in the end, she and Gracelyn chose four pants and four tops whose colors could coordinate, two dresses and one long, more formal dress. The need for the dresses was currently lost on Mara, but she did not question her new friend's suggestions.

They stopped at a shoe store on another level where her feet were scanned before two pairs of footwear were purchased. Their last stop was a small lingerie shop where Mara picked up some lovely essentials. The selections in all of the stores continued to be adequate; a few basic styles and colors to choose from, supplying basic needs without excess. They were assured that the few items which had to be produced would arrive within days. All of the purchased items available for take-away were to be delivered to the house by Helpers or drones, so they were not burdened with any packages as they exited.

On the way back to the main entry Gracelyn said, "That didn't take as long as I thought. Would you like to stop for a cold or hot drink?"

Mara readily agreed, and they turned down a narrow lane lined with artistically appointed windows and a few potted plants. She absently touched one of the plants, surprised to learn it was composed of a stiff construction material. Gracelyn stopped at Bria's Café, where they sat in one of four high-backed booths along the side wall. The only other seating was on stools at a counter, where a man and woman were having a hot drink and talking quietly. Mara looked around and wondered if one of the two working Helpers was named Bria.

They ordered drinks from touch screen menus in their table, and after they arrived Mara asked, "Gracelyn, are you related to Krey?"

"No, but I feel like we could be. Bertie and I arrived on a transport several years ago. We worked on a long voyage with Krey, and now we work here on Cytar whenever we're called. When we met him, we knew he was exceptional. A double house became available, and he asked if we were interested in sharing it. He didn't have to ask us twice. It's a win-win for all of us. We get a great house and neighbor, and we take care of the place and look after Rocket when he's on transport. He's made his place available to others when he's away, but everyone seems to be settled in their own housing."

Mara sipped her hot herbal tea as questions rolled around in her head like Gordian knots, but Gracelyn was already changing the subject to their clothing finds. Eventually, they finished their drinks, and Gracelyn had Mara summon their Gsport on her wrist comm. They meandered back to the entry and the waiting vehicle, passing only two people and one Helper in the quiet open space.

21

Several of the purchases were waiting for them when they arrived home. Mara carried them to her room and hung some on one side of the closet and folded others onto shelves on the other side. She was surprised when she came out to the dining area and found Rocket in the house.

"He comes in now and then," Bertie explained. "He has a large shaded area and a below level house at the side of the yard. He shouldn't be out too long on bright days, and sometimes we spoil him and bring him inside. Truth is, we enjoy having him inside with us."

"Hello Rocket!" Mara greeted him. "Have you had your supper yet?" Bertie was smiling at the dog.

"He has his automatic feed and water station, and he seems to have figured out exactly what time his food appears."

Rocket looked even bigger when he was inside, but he was well behaved, and came right up to Mara for attention. He brought a stuffed toy animal of dubious origin over to show off, before trying to shake it apart. That failing, the dog settled down to try and chew it to a soggy death.

"Somehow, Krey found a new toy for him," Gracelyn said, as she brought steaming dishes to the table.

"Where is Krey?" Mara asked, seeing only three place settings.

"He was called to work. Went out in quite a hurry," Bertie answered. "Happens quite a bit, I'm afraid."

She tried to hide the disappointment that Krey hadn't thought to inform her before he left. The meal of pasta and vegetables was delicious, and the conversation was pleasant. Mara studied them both, trying to determine their age, without success. Bertie had short dark hair, while Gracelyn's wavy brown hair, shorter on the sides and reaching to her collar in back, seemed to proudly exhibit a distinctive, narrow white streak on one side. Both were probably a little older than Krey, and maybe she was slightly younger than all, but that was as far as she could narrow it down.

She helped clear the table while Gracelyn loaded the dishes into the cabinet to be cleaned. Mara called Rocket outside and sat on the settee to enjoy the outdoors. The air was so pure it almost looked like artificial light, but she could tell that the evening light was fleeting, and the darkness was approaching with an eerie abruptness. The temperature was dropping rapidly, but it felt refreshing to be outdoors.

When the cold became uncomfortable, she brought Rocket inside. Krey wasn't home, and Gracelyn and Bertie must have returned to their home, because she had the house to herself. She went into the sitting room, and two wall sconces lighted, giving the room a soft glow. With Rocket padding behind, she decided to further explore the house, starting at the entry door to orientate herself.

On the left was a short adjacent hallway ending with a closed door which opened to the enclosed middle walkway.

Along the right side of this hall were three, near-seamless doors. She remembered that one was the closet where Krey had hung their coats. The second door revealed a narrow closet which housed the program equipment which engaged and monitored the house functions. The third door appeared to be a storage area, and she immediately recognized a smaller version of Mopmop.

She wandered across the narrow entry to the little hall leading to her bedroom and the rooms she hadn't explored. A door next to the bathroom revealed a wash/dry closet. She could see three of Krey's uniform shirts and two pairs of pants through the clear section of the machine. They were hanging and appeared to be clean and dry.

The door to the bedroom next to hers was open. Our room, Krey had said. She looked in at this room, basic, no nonsense, but manly in its austerity. The oversized bed took most of the room, leaving only the narrowest of walk space on either side, and was covered with a simple gray green duvet which flowed into deep blue edges. There was a square, bedside floating shelf with a thinly curved, gray lamp made from the ubiquitous gray metallic material she recognized from her travels. A straight, rather uncomfortable looking chair was the only other piece of furniture. A ground level window looked out to the back and, on the adjacent wall, were two doors. She presumed the closed one to be a closet, and the open door revealed a small bathroom, reminiscent of her "personal room" on the ship.

The door across the hall was also open, but total nightfall was fast approaching, making it difficult to see anything.

"I need some light," she spoke to Rocket as she entered, and a lamp on a flat surface illuminated. This was Krey's office or study, she judged by the flat work area desk and masculine simplicity. This was the smallest of the rooms, but it seemed adequate for its function. There was a window set at an angle, and although the dusk would not reveal a view, she surmised it to be of the open land between the house and town. She was looking at the window when a shade began to lower, apparently prompted by the darkness or outside temperature.

A comfortable looking, cushioned chair sat by the window with a small, low cabinet table nearly touching it. Just a step away, to her right, sat the lighted lamp on the sleek desk, no more than an adjustable flat surface with streamlined legs similar to the ones on the eating table. A cushioned, form-shifting chair was pushed in against the work top. She saw a photo on the opposite wall. Looking closer, she saw that it appeared to be a digital projection of snowcapped mountains in golden and alizarin light. She stared at it for some time, but she could not determine its origin.

Her eyes moved to a shelf, bare except for some sort of a clear, circular shaped art piece. It was an inch thick and stood upright on a flat edge. She picked it up to examine it more closely and was surprised by its substantial weight. When she held it to the light, she could see an etching of a lightning symbol and the word *Superstes* above Krey Kingmore, and, below that, were the numbers 2228. It seemed to be some sort of an award, but not understanding more, she carefully placed it back on the shelf.

Moving to the chair near the window, she picked up a jacket which had been draped across the back and held it to her face, inhaling Krey's lingering scent, masculine and earthy. She sat down with the jacket on her lap, and Rocket came over and settled down at her feet. She felt lonely in the house and was glad to have the dog's company. She put her head back and tried to review all she had seen and learned in her busy day.

When Krey arrived home, the house was quiet. He went to the lighted main room only to find it empty. He was somewhat surprised to see a light on in his office and walked in to find Mara asleep in his chair, covered with his jacket. Rocket, at her feet, gave a couple sheepish tail wags but did not get up.

Krey stood for minute just watching her sleep. Her hair fell partially across her face, and she looked beautiful. A strange feeling washed over him as he looked on the intimate scene of her in his chair with his jacket, and Rocket watching over her. The enormity of his life commitment swept through him, and he suddenly felt a warm emotion from this deeply personal connection. He knelt down and carefully slid the hair off her face.

"Mara," he said softly. "Mara, it's time to get you to bed." He was stroking her hair when she opened her eyes. She looked around, momentarily confused, until she saw his tender smile.

"I was waiting for you. I guess I fell asleep. Is it late?"

"Yes, I'm sorry I didn't call you before I left. I guess I can't be so independent anymore. Let's get you to bed."

He walked her to her room and said good night. She saw the fatigue in his expression and wondered where he had to go in such a hurry.

"Is everything okay?" she asked.

"Yes, it is now. I needed to see something in another area called Ridgeway, and then we had a small ferry shuttle in distress, but we were able to get it in safely. It was bringing home some important supplies we were carrying on board, and we didn't want to lose them or the crew and shuttle. It was hectic for a while, but it's all good now" He gave her a quick hug. "Sleep well. I'll see you in the morning."

She would need a good sleep to face the new information she would have to process the following day.

22

The following morning, when Mara came into the eating area, Gracelyn was getting ready to leave.

"Oh, I'm glad I caught you. Bertie and I were called in, and we're off to work today, so you're on your own for breakfast. Coffee's made for you. You can find where things are, so help yourself to anything. I'll see you later. You know how to call if you need anything, and Krey's around here somewhere."

"Thanks Gracelyn. I'll be fine. Have a good day."

Another bright day beckoned, so Mara placed a slice of the grainy bread in the all-cook and requested toast, poured a cup of coffee and went out to eat on the patio. Rocket was out and raced over to greet her.

"I'm guessing you've already eaten." The energetic dog responded by taking a racing circle around the yard while she settled herself in the chair.

It was very pleasant outside and exceptionally quiet. After she finished the toast, she meandered slowly through the yard with her coffee cup in her hand, looking, without success, for birdlife or a flying insect. So strangely quiet. She inspected the few plants more closely, but the different forms and leaf shapes were not familiar to her. On closer inspection she noticed the unique leaf structure, with the thick tough underside. The miniature plants were huddled together as if there were safety in numbers from the intimidating weather. The stunted looking growth was clinging close to the ground and fighting to put out small leaves. The two under-nourished looking shrubs appeared to have a hardscrabble life, and the short dense trees stubbornly grew, apparently despite the whipsaw changes in day and night temperatures. Even the soil seemed different. It was coarse in places, almost granular, and sometimes, when catching the light just right, shown with iridescence.

When she returned to the kitchen, she heard Krey's voice coming from his office. She quietly walked to the door and looked in. He was standing with his back to her, using an air screen and talking to someone. She observed him, working confidently in control, in his element. He looked so handsome, not pretty boy handsome, but strong handsome, intelligent handsome, ruggedly handsome, where all the parts of his face and strong jaw went together in just the right way. Watching him, she was suddenly struck by how little she knew about this man and this place. It was at that moment that he finished his call, flipped his hand to close the screen and turned to see her standing in the doorway. Their eyes met, and his smile filled her with warm emotions which pushed aside her unknowns. He walked over and gave her a quick hug.

"Good morning." He almost didn't recognize his own happy sentiments, but they grew when he looked at her and thought of this exciting new and unfolding permanent relationship. They wandered out to the main room.

"How would you like to visit my work hub today?"

"I'd like that very much. I don't know much about any of the jobs around here, but Gracelyn and Bertie were called in to work today."

"Yes, I spoke with them before they left. I'm guessing you'll be offered some work soon, too, if you're interested," he said.

Mara was surprised. "I'm not sure what I could do, but I'm willing to try, and I'd like to learn whatever they need me to do."

"Have no fear. You'll be surprised at how much you already know. You're a fast learner, and the training will be excellent." He projected a sureness and strength which again made her feel both protected and confident.

Later that morning, they left the house in the Gsport and headed toward the Gateway Complex on a dazzlingly bright day. The vehicle windows tinted to reduce the glare as Mara scanned the brown landscape. The plant life was quite limited. No lush green scenery here. For a second time, she noticed a small, low structure near some little, clingy trees, which looked like they were trying to hide for protection. She asked about the tiny building.

"That's a survival pod. We have several scattered around the perimeter of our complex."

She was intrigued. "What are they for?"

"As you've noticed, our weather can be treacherous. If someone happens to be caught outside when night falls or an unexpected storm erupts, it can be deadly. The best chance to survive is to shelter in one of those pods until the storm abates or morning comes with warmer temperatures."

Mara remained quiet in thought as they approached the Complex, but the vehicle continued past and circled around to an area she had not seen with Gracelyn. They entered an underground tunnel and drove lower and slower.

The Gsport announced, "You are arriving at Station One," as they came to a stop. They exited their vehicle and entered a doorway.

They approached a second door which opened after a voice stated, "K2203.10.21 and M2209.7.14, Gate One."

The third door opened with "Ten point two one, and Seven point one four, cleared."

They continued through a passage which sloped gently downward until they came to a wide door which opened on their approach. They entered an open area with smaller clear-walled work stations surrounding it. A few were occupied with two or three workers who seemed busy on projects and barely took notice of them. Various shaped chairs in different configurations sat in the open area. One chair in a reclined position was occupied by a man studying a hologram floating above him.

One of the doors along the side opened unexpectedly, and Captain Lor walked out with a big grin. "Krey, great to see you here!

"Hello, Lor, I wasn't expecting to see you here; it's a nice surprise. I don't believe you've been formally introduced to

Mara. Mara, this is the skillful captain that brought our ship close enough to bring our docking transports into Cytar."

"Hello, Mara. I remember you from the expedition, and I'm so happy that you're with Krey. He needs someone to keep him in line," Lor said jokingly.

"It's nice to meet you," Mara smiled as she replied, although she was still not sure she understood this new information about the ship and docking transports.

"Perhaps we'll get to know each other a bit more at the appreciation dinner that is being planned for some time next week. You're planning on coming, aren't you?" He was directing his question to Krey.

"We'll be there, don't worry. Now, I'm going to meet someone at programming and show Mara around a bit."

They said goodbyes, and Lor watched them walk away, smiling as he noticed the happy demeanor in his first officer's body language. Krey led Mara to a partitioned workspace where a worker was studying on a reader. Krey gave a quick knock on the clear wall.

"Excuse me, Idwarda. Do you have a minute?"

The woman looked up, and her eyes flicked quickly from Krey's wrist to Mara's and back to Krey.

She smiled. "Of course, always for you, Krey. It was good to get your call, and welcome back! The entire population is beyond happy that everyone is home safely."

"Thanks, but probably not as happy as we are. I'd like you to meet Mara, from the *Superstes*. Mara, this is Idwarda, a topnotch coder and all-around AI specialist." There was a brief exchange of hellos and comments about his expedition before Krey got to the point.

"We've spoken about the bonding algorithms, and I was wondering if you'd had a chance to look them over."

"Yes, I've looked through pretty much all of the section you were concerned about, and only found one possible little glitch. Come, have a look."

She tapped her reader and a square of light hung before them like a sheer curtain.

"Let's get this unfolded so you can review it for yourself. Block, life pledge; Function, conduct." Lines of code began rolling in the light frame until she pointed and stopped it at one piece saying, "I've changed one small part here which slightly changes the weighting of the conduct information. That's the only thing we could find that would have caused the apparent poor life match. Either that, or it could be that the crew member was having some minor issues during travel but ordinarily would have been fine."

Krey skewed up one side of his face as if he wasn't sure of her last comment. He started carefully reading the highlighted unit, line per line.

"This is where I changed the weighting," Idwarda said pointing to a specific area. "I've sent it for review and approval."

Krey, at last, seemed satisfied. "Thank you, this looks good. I know that took some time and energy, and I appreciate your help."

"Not a problem," she answered. "I had Helpers working with me, and most of this is as self-generating as we allow it to be. Besides, you know how fast all this works with these big networks incorporating time crystals."

"I know, Idwarda. We're all aware that it's played a big part in the reason we can be here and accomplish all we've done. Yeah, and the speed of the qubit messaging in our networks is breathtaking, thanks to the work and brain power of people like you. It used to be the same game drilled into everyone, right? I remember, as I'm sure you do, all the old stories we heard of the discussions and research on better ways to manipulate and transfer huge amounts of data rapidly, using less space and generating less heat. I know data storage and transmission speed is a never-ending focus of people like you and the technology teams. All of us here have great respect for all of you."

"Oh, we all remember those old stories about the old wi-fi. Just don't forget that we have our share of hiccups and setbacks like everyone else, but some of these people I work with are the amazing ones. Talk about mathematical and techie brainpower; we're lucky to have them, but then again, thank goodness everyone has a different talent or we wouldn't be here." She pointed back to the changed area.

"The software is writing its own code now to test this little change. When it's done, they'll run some archived data through and check it against prior successful matches. Shouldn't take too long. Matching errors could be a disaster which would put the whole bonding process in jeopardy, so it's good that you brought up the concern."

"Well, I'm glad you and your team are able to understand and keep up with the constant updates and changes. And I think all the matches seem to be working out fine," he said, looking at Mara.

She had been watching intently, taking in the conversations and following along. Most of the technology references flowed in her mind, but a question lingered from Lor's conversation.

After they left the room, she was quiet for a few moments before she asked, "What did you mean when you were talking to Captain Lor, and you mentioned something about docking transports? Didn't we just dock our ship when we landed before that storm?"

"Not quite. The *Superstes* is too large to safely dock here. She stays out, and we ferry in and out to her."

She knew that the memories of the hectic, fast moving last day on the ship were fluid in her brain.

Still bothered, she asked, "Where is the ferry we traveled on?"

Krey laughed. "You have the questions, don't you? Come on, I'll show you." He led her to a mover which descended one level while traveling.

They exited and went to a small room. Krey touched the wall and a section became a transparent window. The sight before her left Mara speechless.

23

They were looking at an enormous enclosed space, but it was the unique vehicle near the center of the expanse which was overwhelming Mara. This was no ocean vessel, no deep-sea traveler, no short distance air transport. Three workers, each with a Helper, looked dwarfed by this transport's size. One end narrowed and flattened while the other broadened. The four relatively small angular sweptback wing-like projections hugged its body, and she could distinguish no windows on the fuselage. It was sitting on massive low cradling rods which extended the length of the cavernous building.

Krey could not read the disturbed look on Mara's face, but he had the alarming thought of having made a significant mistake. She didn't speak for over a minute while he worried, thinking, now too late, of her lack of wake-up medications and her memory gaps.

"This is what we call the C-transport because we traveled on it from the *Superstes* to Cytar," he tried to explain.

Silence.

"Where am I?" she finally said, almost demanding. A dull throb in her brain was looming.

He was desperately thinking of something to say without further upsetting her.

Finally, he said, "We're on Cytar, a place that is new to you. Your home was too dangerous to stay, so we brought you here. This will be a better home for us, and we'll be together here."

Silence.

She kept staring, trying to understand. The Gordian knots were returning to her mixed-up thoughts. Nothing in her strange journey completely made sense, and now she was desperately trying to reconcile this new information. She kept blinking as if that would clear her head. Not knowing what to do, Krey simply took her hand and didn't say anything. She kept holding his hand tightly, which he took as a good sign.

At last, he turned. "Come, I think we should go now, maybe get something to eat," he said in an attempt to placate her.

He led her to a mover, but she no longer paid any attention to where it was taking them. They emerged into a bright area, which she recognized from her trip with Gracelyn. He took her down one of the pleasant lanes and stopped at a busy café. A Helper led them to a table overlooking the open middle area of the complex. Mara sat with a blank look while he looked at a menu in the table.

"The food here is more typical for us. Gracelyn procured some special fresh food to celebrate our return. This food will be better than on the transport, but not as good as Gracelyn's. It's all very nutritious," he added lamely, wishing she would say something. "Do you see something you'd like?" he finally asked, hopefully.

"I'm not very hungry," she said, pointing at last to a picture of a bowl of vegetable soup.

"Good choice," he said, thankful she wasn't going berserk. This outing was not going as he had planned. Their order arrived, but it was a quiet lunch with Krey trying to carry the conversation between bites of his vegetables and protein. His appetite was all but gone, and she barely touched her order.

Mara finally asked, "Where are Cali and Buddy?"

Krey, who had been waiting on tenterhooks, looked relieved by the simple question.

"AI pets stay on the main transport ship. Cali arrived with us. She's actually with Gracelyn or Bertie right now. They check, overhaul, update or repair Helpers. Cali will be perfect when they're finished with her."

She smiled as if picturing Cali and Buddy in her mind. He breathed a sigh of relief. *Thank you, God, for her normal smile.*

"Have you seen Genna or Omi?"

"No, I'm not sure where they live. In one of the apartments, I imagine. I'll bet we see them at the appreciation dinner."

Her face brightened. "I hope so."

After lunch they walked through the complex for a long while. He was in no hurry to be home alone with Mara if she was still upset. He thought he had done enough damage to the day and was worried he would say something which might add to her distress. He reasoned that being out and seeing people going about their lives normally could be more soothing to her. They window shopped, but he could not interest her in going into any of the small stores. They sat on a bench for some time, not talking, just watching the calm activity of the place. He held her hand as if he didn't want to lose her.

At last, he said, "Wait here a minute, please. There's something I want to get."

He walked into a nearby shop and returned after a few minutes with a smile on his face.

"I think we need to get back."

Mara remained very quiet and subdued the rest of the day. That night, after an almost silent dinner, Krey brought out the long coats and led Mara up into the yard.

"I think you need to see this spectacle of our night sky. Maybe it will help you to understand your journey," he said as they looked up at the incomprehensible number of stars in the dark perfectly clear atmosphere.

She had seen stars at night before, but never had she seen this number with such brilliance. They looked closer than she had ever seen them, and they felt as if she could almost reach out and touch them. There were no bright lights interfering with the intense expansive view. It was as if someone had magnified the heavens and allowed her to see deep into space. Stars upon stars were everywhere she looked, with a distinct cluster of them shedding spectacular brilliance. She recognized no constellations. For a moment she was overwhelmed at the immensity of it all, and she felt small. He didn't speak, wanting her to have her own thoughts.

Moments passed before she turned to him and said in a quiet voice, "There are no oceans here, are there?"

"No," was all he answered.

She shivered. The temperature was dropping rapidly, but she didn't move, and he dared not rush her.

In a voice barely above a whisper she asked, "How far "out" is the *Superstes* now?"

"Under normal circumstances it takes the C-transport almost a full day to depart Cytar, reach her and dock. Because of the upcoming weather event we traveled faster, which for safety, necessitated the suits and head gear. Our ship will remain out there in orbit, be updated, retrofitted and possibly remodeled or repaired, until needed for long voyage travel. In the meantime, it will be used for space monitoring, experiments and important scientific research as well as storage for life saving supplies in the event of a catastrophe here. If we were outside at night at the right time, we could see her faint light move in its orbit across the sky." She stood still for a long minute, looking up at the universe above her.

Finally, she nodded her head in a solemn resignation and said, "I'd like to go in now."

She didn't speak when they were inside, merely handed him her coat and walked to the hall. He went into the sitting room and sat down, still holding the coats. What had happened to this mixed-up day? It started out full of happiness, and he ended up baffled by what was going on in Mara's head, wondering if he had ruined everything. All he wanted was for them to be happy together and make a good life in this unforgiving, bleak place.

He sighed deeply and quietly said, "Wall images."

His saved images began randomly cycling in front of him. He almost immediately saw what he wanted and pointed, sending an enlarged photo image to the entire wall across from him. The clear picture displayed a pure, deep blue lake being watched over by craggy, snowcapped mountains. Strong, tall evergreens framed the picture, stalwarts guarding the entrance to spiritual beauty. He stared at the large image for some time, his eyes moving around and throughout the scene. The strength and quietness of the sight usually gave clarity to his thoughts, but tonight so many concerns weighed on his mind, it did little to change his mood before he eventually closed it.

That night, when he went to his room, he found her curled up in his bed hugging his pillow. She felt him gently take the pillow, felt his arms wrap around her like a comforting shield, protecting her vulnerability from this incomprehensible space above them. She could not yet understand all the circumstances in this new world, but she understood kindness, caring and passionate feelings.

He held her closely and stroked her hair. She kept her head near his shoulder with her hand on his chest. This felt right; this was where she felt safe. He couldn't read her thoughts, and he knew there were few words which could help her to comprehend all she had seen today. His desire was to convey his growing love for her, which he did in the most tender and intimate way he knew.

24

The next few days were a mine field of emotions as Mara sorted the divergent feelings which came from realizing she was in a totally new environment and yet, still unable to draw on memories of events prior to her journey. Everything would now need to be reviewed through a new understanding of her reality. She was quieter than normal, creating days which were a bit strained, but Krey remained steadfast in his support. Gracelyn, Bertie and Krey often had to leave in the morning for work at various sites. Mara, now left alone, needed to avoid the affliction of overthinking the circumstances in her new world. She filled her time with reading, and she began to find more articles about several of the jobs worked on during travel.

Exercise helped clear her mind and pass the time. The long walks with Rocket, the occasional runs, and the exertion all helped to sort out her new revelations. Bertie had shown her how to put special goggles on the dog if she planned to be out with him more than an hour. Rocket must have been accustomed to this protective gear because he ignored the goggles and was always anxious to go for a walk.

The seemingly endless light of a particularly cloudless day beckoned, and she was drawn outdoors, meandering through the winding pathways between the spaciously placed houses in their small community, until she stopped to study the strange looking little dwellings. Two of the houses looked exactly like Krey's, and three appeared to be even smaller, but they all had the narrow middle walkways suggesting two households in each structure.

On a brilliant day like today, when the light drenched the long side of the solar rooftops, they shone beautifully with a copper-like sheen, making a crisp contrast to the earth-toned walls. The metal wind cylinders on the roofs' peaks curved over the edges like a sculpture of rolling waves. A strange climate, she reflected as she scanned the area, so glacially cold at night with intense daytime light which produced only moderate heat. But this strange place somehow produced a near-Earth atmosphere which contained just enough oxygen to support them.

After winding through the sparse vegetation in the neighborhood, she continued out into the country, always looking for bird or animal life, but save for some infrequent plant life, the land appeared barren. The clear panorama seemed limitless and was soundless except for their soft, crunching footfalls. She discovered that the ground was not as flat as it had had seemed from a distance. There were numerous rocks of all shapes and sizes on uneven ground, and the sparse plant life all but disappeared as she travelled further from the houses. She worried that Rocket could cut his feet on some of the sharper rocks, but this dog, a happy clunk indoors who never seemed to know where his tail was flapping, was now the epitome of agility in motion, choosing his path carefully without injury.

She was quite a distance from the house when she felt the inexplicable need to just stop and stand to absorb and attempt to connect with this vast expanse of nothingness. This was her new home, but as far as she could see there was nothing but brown dirt. Brown dirt with sharp depressions, a few low bluffs in the distance and nothingness. She and Rocket were the only two living beings detected in the entire silent, huge and treacherous vastness before them. A gust of wind rippled through her hair, and in the distance, two vertical, swirling wind tunnels danced and played with each other, moving up and down, gathering dirt as they twirled off.

Standing there alone, the land felt powerful, and she felt vulnerable facing it. No competition here, no question of the winner in a survival contest. This desolate land wins, no doubt, as it had for eons of time. She turned back and saw the peculiar looking little abodes, half buried and hanging on to the land, hunkered down as if ready for the next combat against the elements. Further still, the Gateway complex looked insignificant and only visible despite its remoteness because of the pure atmosphere.

The danger of a monotonous landscape became evident when she decided to venture further ahead.

"Come on, Rocket. Let's see what's over that small bluff."

The dog bolted ahead, curious to explore what was beyond. They crested the ridge and made their way down through more uneven terrain until she realized that, aside from the ground becoming more jagged, the view was not improved. When she turned to head home, she was disturbed to realize she had lost all land markers. Her group of houses and Gateway were nowhere in sight. She turned around and saw the same vista in every direction. She studied the view until she thought she recognized the bluff, but the climb to the top revealed only more desolation. Moments of panic overtook her when realized how easily one could become disoriented and become lost in this unforgiving, deadly environment. Her thoughts turned to her wrist comm, hoping it could direct her to the house.

"Map home base," she said, waiting for what seemed to be too long.

At last, a small, pale blinking dot appeared on the screen. She started in the direction she thought it indicated, only to see the blinking light disappear. Turning around, she navigated the flashing image by trial and error until her wrist comm began auditory directions, and Gateway came into the distant view, giving her the needed visual bearing. She vowed to learn how to better use the mapping features and not to mention this little, but potentially disastrous, misadventure.

The sheer desolation of the experience kindled thoughts of the refreshing green outdoor area Krey had taken her to on their ship. It was truly astounding that such a micro ecosystem could be sustained on that ship. Those awe-inspiring experiences created the smallest seed of an idea. It sat, as all seeds do, waiting for favorable conditions to sprout.

Back in her small safe dwelling, she marveled at the comforts which the Cytar pioneers had created in such a new and hostile land. They had built small, but solid shelters and infrastructures, which essentially provided for all the basic needs and more for survival.

Her solo adventure had produced a good appetite, so she put Rocket back in his shelter and headed to the eating room. She examined the choices from the food menu, chose a meal packet in its edible wrapping, and had the all-cook prepare it. The balance of protein and carbohydrates would contain the appropriate calories for her body. She ate slowly, looking out the back clear door, thinking that someday she would like to invite Gracelyn and Bertie over for dinner. They were good people, and she felt fortunate to have them in her life.

25

By chance, Krey came home early the very next afternoon and decided to check the food inventory of the frozen cabinet. He was pleasantly surprised to hear rabbit announced in the list, and silently thanked Gracelyn for ordering and saving the prized protein. As if hearing Mara's thoughts, he suggested they prepare this special meal together and share it with their neighbors. Their diet had been gradually changing from the delicious fresh food Gracelyn had purchased for their homecoming, to the more normal packages of prepared proteins, basic grains, vegetables and limited fruits. The rabbit meat would be a culinary treat, and they agreed to personally prepare a feast for Gracelyn and Bertie. Besides, Krey was hoping that having a common purpose would be a good way for both of them to be together without causing any unusual questions to arise.

They actually found themselves joking and enjoying the task. They laughed over little things, like Rocket's antics, or because neither could ever remember where anything was kept in the prep area, and especially because they ultimately realized that they just did not know what they were doing. At one point, Krey's joking triggered something inside Mara, causing the wonderful uncontrollable laughter which comes from a release of pent-up emotions. Tears of contagious laughter were filling her eyes, and their shared laughter broke some unexplainable tension which had grown between them.

"We have quite the domestic skills, especially for food prep," Krey finally said, teasingly.

"More like a total lack of skills, and if we keep going, I'm thinking Rocket will be eating rabbit tonight." Mara chided, but he could see she was having fun and seemed more like herself.

"Real meat is way too valuable for that."

He was studying the all-cook now as if it were quantum physics. Mara walked over, said "rabbit," and looked over the choices presented. Following one of the suggestions, she placed the rabbit in cookware with some vegetables and an herbal sauce packet and told the appliance to braise the meal.

The final decision proved to be the surest method, and they were pleased with the tender meat and flavorful carrots and potatoes. Their neighbors were pleasantly surprised and grateful for the meal and the company. At one point, Bertie and Gracelyn, without verbal communication, acknowledged through a knowing glance at each other, the positive changes in the more relaxed and talkative newly-committed couple. As they were finishing Krey said, "Tomorrow night, Mara and I are going to the expedition appreciation dinner."

"Oh, we heard about that at work, "Bertie said. "It's been a popular topic of conversation."

"It will be a lovely affair, I'm sure, if it's like the one we attended the year we returned from a long voyage," Gracelyn chimed in.

"Mara, you'll get to wear your new dress."

"Will everyone from the ship be there?" Mara asked.

"Everyone is invited, and I'm sure the turnout will be excellent," Krey said. "I'm sure you'll see people from your group."

The next day, Mara's mood lightened as she anticipated seeing her friends from the voyage. That evening, she dressed carefully in the cobalt blue ankle length gown she and Gracelyn had picked out. It was sleeveless with a V neck and an open back. She took extra time with her hair, sweeping it up on one side, and then slipped into her heel strapped shoes, took a deep breath and walked out into the hall.

Krey, dressed in the formal uniform he wore at the bonding ceremony, was just coming out of his office and stopped when he saw her. Their eyes met, and they smiled.

"I have a gift for you," he said, walking up to her.

He opened a small box which displayed a headband made of small beautifully cut crystals. He led her to the entry mirror, and she watched as he carefully placed the narrow band. It was positioned half way to her left ear, but continued down past her right ear, forming a beautiful pendant earring, now with two lines of jewels hanging just below the ear. The dark hair was a perfect contrast to the shimmering gems, and the effect was stunning.

"Thank you, it's so gorgeous," she said, feeling how close he was and how good that felt. His face was near hers, and he kissed her softly.

"You are beautiful."

She stood motionless, looking into his eyes, emotional from the kiss and not wanting to spoil the moment.

He paused, letting his eyes take in her face and hair and jewelry, before finally saying, "We should go."

They put on their long coats and hurried to the waiting Gsport.

26

They traveled through a gentle and welcome rain until their vehicle brought them to the event through a different Complex tunnel entrance. A Helper took their coats, and they joined a short line of couples, each of whom had their names announced before proceeding. Mara's hand was linked through Krey's arm when they stopped, and a voice stated, "Krey and Mara Kingmore," before they merged into a large lively group in the well-lit banquet hall. The initial overheard chatter seemed to be focusing on the rare rain, which added to the group's good spirits.

"I don't know about the name Kingmore," Mara started, remembering the art piece in Krey's study, but he interrupted.

"I know, I know, more questions. We'll talk on the way home, but right now I want to enjoy myself with my beautiful woman."

Mara scanned the room of men is dress uniforms and women in lovely flowing gowns until she saw Genna and Omi talking together.

"I see my friends. I'd like to go see them."

"Go on. I'll find a Helper and get us a drink and catch up with you."

The women exchanged hugs and shared the girl talk compliments on their hair and dresses, with admiring comments on Mara's headband.

"Thank you, a gift from Krey. You both look great and happy. What's been going on with you since we left the ship?" Mara asked, eager to catch up on news.

Omi answered first. "Things are going well and we're very busy. Lan and I have a nice little apartment in this contained complex. It has two rooms!" She emphasized the two, as if to accentuate its massiveness.

"I live in an apartment pod with two other girls from the ship," Genna added. "Omi and I run across each other now and then, and we had lunch together last week." Her smile widened as she added, "and I met someone at work I really like. I want you to meet him soon."

The women were very interested in the village, as they called it, where Mara and Krey lived. She had never thought of the little group of buildings as a village, but she described her home and said they needed to meet there someday for a tour.

"It will take me all of five minutes to show you our home and walk around the area," she laughed, "but we can go for a hike and visit, and it'll be wonderful to stay connected."

They continued talking almost all at once, until Lan arrived with drinks for Genna and Omi.

"Hello, Mara, nice to see you. I didn't know you were here or I'd have brought you a drink, too. Can I get you something?"

"Hello Lan, great to see you. No worries, Krey is bringing me a drink, thanks," she said, just as he arrived with icy, citrus-infused drinks.

They toasted to their reunion and visited briefly before a dinner announcement was made, and all began migrating to their seats. Krey and Mara were at a front table with Captain Lor, his spouse, and Dr. Tanak and another woman. The captain was obviously glad to be home, demonstrated by the affection he was showing to his attractive wife. With arms around each other, they had been talking and laughing with several people and mingling throughout the room before taking their seats. Mara was seated between Dr. Tanak and Krey.

"Mara, it's so good to see you and see how good you and Krey look together," Tanak said. "I'd like you to meet my friend, Liella."

A pretty woman with the same brow line and thin eyebrows as Tanak greeted Mara warmly. Everyone exchanged small talk as dinner was served. It was a truly festive meal with a piece of chicken in an herbal sauce served with quinoa and fresh vegetables, and a soft dinner roll which everyone quickly devoured. Dessert was a small dish of sliced fresh fruit which Mara decided must be very special by the pleased reaction of the diners.

When she had the chance, she asked Tanak, "Do you live in the complex?"

"Oh no, I don't live in Gateway; I live on the other side in Ridgeway. I could have a house, but since I'm single, I prefer the convenience of an apartment."

"Is that far from here?" she inquired.

"We came in my ground transport, in rapid mode of course, and it still took over two hours. A speed tunnel was started years ago, but when we lost the *Navigator*, we had to pull all Helpers to work on other manufacturing projects. Someday, we'll get back to it, and then it will save hours of travel between all sites. Our complexes were built where we found the most habitable place with adequate ground water, and I'm afraid that seems to be in short supply on Cytar. Actually, water seems to have been a constant source of concern throughout humanity. We are trying to be responsible stewards of such a precious resource."

Mara nodded, listening intently, and took a sip of her drink as Tanak continued. "They built three separate living complexes here to protect against total annihilation in case of some catastrophic event, hoping, I guess, that at least one place would survive. At any rate, we're grateful for a place with sustainable atmosphere, so we won't complain. I doubt there is another planet with our extreme night temperatures and yet also has somewhat moderate daylight temperatures. We're very fortunate."

"Yes, remarkably fortunate. Will you be returning home tonight?"

"No, we're staying in one of the overnight rooms. It's not really that smart to travel at night unless there's an emergency and then, if necessary, only in one of the heavy-duty vehicles. The nighttime temperatures are so extreme they could be life threatening if one had a transport problem."

The conversations continued amicably as more questions stacked up in Mara's brain. The stimulation from so many people in one place ricocheted in her head, while she tried to take in sights of all the crew and Candidates. She noticed several couples with matching wrist marks similar to hers and Krey's.

He ordered another round of the refreshing drinks before Helpers cleared plates, and Captain Lor gave a brief but heartfelt speech thanking his crew for their exceptional work.

He started by joking about how the crew practically forced him to travel through dangerous weather events because they were so tired of being with him. He transitioned smoothly into a serious manner, seamlessly weaving his dialogue into a paean of well-deserved and much appreciated praise for their successful mission. He gave Tanak and Krey special recognition for their invaluable and tireless efforts in keeping the ship and team safe.

Mara looked out at the crew and saw the esteem they reflected for their captain, and she understood their respect. Lor had that innate leadership quality that combined his knowledge and decisiveness while projecting care and trust. His speech was well received and appreciated.

Afterwards, everyone started getting up and talking, and music soon began to play in the background. Mara turned quickly to look for its source, fascinated by the group of three men and two women playing instruments. She made her way over until she was standing near them. Krey followed her, interested in her reaction.

"I recognize the saxophone and guitar, but I can't think of the names of other instruments. I think the festivities and all the interactions with people are confusing me," she said lightly.

"That one is an oboe, a flute and a violin," he pointed as he named them. "We only have a precious few of these authentic instruments, and they aren't brought out very often, but we are trying to keep music alive. A few of our citizens are teaching the skills to others. Music is good for the brain, either in learning it or listening to it. We know that the different beats and cadences affect the mind and body differently. We often use this knowledge on long voyages to help stimulate or calm the mind. We have all the new music technologies, but we are trying not to lose our humanity to technology and become like Helpers. We're hoping the old musical instruments will help us with that goal."

So engrossed in watching and listening to the musicians, she was only partly absorbing what he was saying. She did not notice that many couples were dancing behind them, until Krey guided her out and began the slow dance with her. Something in her past responded to the rhythms and his direction, and she became lost in the music. Krey held her close to him as she leaned in, and they moved together to the gentle melody.

The evening flowed with the perfect balance of music, dancing and visiting. At one point, while Krey was talking to a fellow crew member, Mara decided to circulate on her own and visit acquaintances from her voyage. She was making her way through the crowd when Draven walked in front of her.

"Well, hello Mara," he said, but she could not read his tone. *Surely no problems here.* "So nice to see you again," he went on smoothly. "I'm sorry things didn't work out for us. I was hoping you would honor me with one dance."

Without waiting for a reply, he took her hand and led her to an open spot and began dancing with her. He held her too closely for her comfort, but when she tried to create a little space between them, he applied more pressure to her back.

"This is nice," he said, while Mara put on an unfeeling smile and tried to stay composed. Luckily, they had joined part way into the dance, and as soon as the music stopped, she broke away with a quick "nice to see you again." She walked away as she scanned the room for someone she could join. She found Krey, who noticed her more serious expression.

"Is everything all right?" She tried to give him a reassuring smile and a nod as she looked around.

"Just getting tired, I think."

They left soon after as others began to depart. Amid hugs, Omi and Genna promised to get together soon. Captain Lor was standing at the exit door with two Helpers. He personally thanked each crew member by name for their service on the voyage, shook their hand, and presented each with a clear, circular recognition award similar to the one Mara had seen in Krey's office. So, she realized, this was his second long voyage. She looked at the art piece and saw the lightning symbol above the inscription.

Superstes

Krey Kingmore

2233

They hurried into their Gsport and left the complex in the midst of fierce gusts of wind which peppered driving sleet into the windshield. The vehicle was immediately buffeted by the angry weather, but quickly adjusted its powered gyroscopes for a smoother ride.

As soon as the ride settled, Mara began. "So, tell me about the name Kingmore. Why haven't I ever heard anyone use that name before?"

Krey started laughing. "I knew the questions would be coming. Yes, that is officially my complete name, which is rarely used. These settlements were so small in the early years, second names were hardly needed, and that habit of first name use has largely continued. Plus, our crew on the transport is so small we rarely need more. We usually are identified by our first name or the last digits of our code; it often works the same in all three communities, and you've seen my code numbers on our electronic communications as well."

"Where does Captain Lor live?" was her next question.

"He lives in the Apogeeway Complex. It's the furthest from us and has a little more vegetation than ours, thanks to slightly more ground water. I heard you talking to Tanak about Ridgeway, so now you know all three of our habitation complexes. They are similar to the one we live in, but I would still love to show them to you some day."

"I'd like that very much."

Before she could ask another question, the Gsport announced their arrival home. It had been a pleasant evening for Krey, seeing his friends and crew and especially being able to share it with Mara.

Except for the brief, slightly uncomfortable encounter with Draven, Mara thought the event was wonderful. She felt pride as she more fully appreciated Krey's role in their successful journey and looked forward to connecting again with friends.

She kicked off her shoes while Krey hung up the coats, and they went down the hall together. When they reached their bedroom door, he took her hand and looked into her eyes, struggling again to compose the words which would convey his feelings for her. In the end he just led her into the room and closed the door to finish what he had started with his earlier kiss.

27

After making a pot of coffee, Gracelyn was looking out on a gray, overcast morning. There was still evidence of the previous evening's storm, and a few droplets of moisture still hung like jewelry from plants, a result of the melting frost from the frigid night, now retreating in the pale morning light, but staying obstinately strong in the shadows. Mesmerizing mists of vapor rose in random swirls from the thick tree trunks and branches. She turned when she heard Krey enter the room and watched him head straight for the coffee.

"You look happy on one of our grayer days. The dinner must have been quite the gala affair."

"It was very nice, good food, good music, and a great turnout. Mara got to see her friends and meet lots of people."

"I'm glad for her. She must be sleeping in."

"No, I'm up. Good morning, Gracelyn," Mara said as she entered the room, but she was smiling at Krey, who brought her a cup of coffee with his own meaningful smile. Gracelyn raised her eyebrows. *Hmm, yes, things are going very well.*

"What an unusually gray morning," Mara remarked as she stepped outside with her coffee. The soil was still damp with tiny telltale rivulet tracks on the ground where the water had trickled until it seeped underground. For the first time she thought she noticed a few miniscule insects wandering on the surface, but they disappeared quickly and, without a closer inspection, she wondered if she had imagined them. The air felt humid, and the sky was a solid, undescriptive gray. She held the coffee cup in both hands, enjoying its warmth and not minding the grayness or the chill. It was still invigorating just being outside after her confined travel time.

Once they were alone, Gracelyn spoke to Krey. "I just came in this morning to make sure you're both feeling settled. Bertie and I don't plan to be coming over as often now that Mara's found her way around the place."

For a moment Krey looked as if he was about to lose his best friends. "Gracelyn, you and Bertie are always welcome here, at any time. Do you know what a sight for sore eyes you were when I got home? And I don't think Mara and I would have made it without both of you here. I know that you have your own lives, and I don't want you to feel as if you have to babysit us, but I want you to be a part of our lives, just as you've always been."

Gracelyn laughed, "Don't worry, we're only next door. We'll see each often enough. We're just glad you're back safely, and you have Mara with you now. I think you two are good for each other." She gave Krey a reassuring hug before she returned to her house.

Mara was returning to the dining area when her wrist comm indicated a message.

"I'm invited to attend an employment workshop this afternoon at Gate 2." Her eyes were bright with interest. "I don't know where Gate 2 is."

"Our ground transport knows, but I'll be going in to work on-site today, so I can drop you off and see that you get to the right place. It's nice that you're in one of the first groups to be called in."

They left the house after lunch, and within minutes, the gray skies surrendered to a fresh brilliance. Krey pointed in the distance to a large circular depression holding a small pond, which looked as if it were ready to be swallowed by the thirsty soil.

"That basin was built to capture rain water and gradually send it below to underground reservoirs. We have several on Cytar because our climate goes through so many unpredictable arid spells, and we need the basins to provide a more reliable water supply. We get very few measurable rainfalls a year."

"There's so much I don't know, and so much I can't seem to remember," Mara commented as she watched the landscapes slide past.

"Well, you're probably going to learn a lot at this meeting today," he said as the vehicle stopped at Gate 2. He started to walk her to the entry, but a Helper was ready to greet her. He pointed to his wrist comm and said, "Let me know when you're finished, and I'll pick you up."

28

A Helper led her to a room with four rectangular work tables, each with three chairs. Except for a small digital sign on the wall which read, "All work is honorable," the walls were bare. Nine other former Candidates were invited to the workshop, which was led by a serious looking woman who introduced herself simply as Zoe. Mara recognized her fellow travelers from the voyage. Greetings and small talk immediately began, but Zoe got right down to business.

"Please find your seat at one of the stations, and welcome to Gateway's introduction workshop. Everyone is excited and very grateful to have you here. Today, I'll give you a brief overview of our habitation complex and explain some of our job needs. The work which has been accomplished to create what we have here, and what you are about to see, is outstanding. The level of colonization is truly remarkable, thanks to the selfless efforts of our citizens."

A large map of their complex appeared on a wall image behind Zoe. Mara was surprised at the different sections displayed. She saw where the entrances to the complex were located. The offices Krey had showed her and the Cytar transport work station were more distant than she realized. She made a mental note of how rapidly underground movers must travel. There were three outlying areas which were unknown to her, and she noticed that the Gateway Complex was the central hub, with the other work locations radiating out like spokes on a wheel.

Zoe was talking about the map and pointing to the areas outside of the complex.

"This large area is our power plant. We use several power sources at Gateway, but our station, with its huge need, uses nuclear power. The plant contains two small reactors, although we have other energy circuitry and sources for our small work units and devices here." She highlighted a long, flat slightly curved building. "This uniquely shaped building converts wind to energy."

She pointed out another area, "and this large facility is our manufacturing and repair center, which we hope to continually expand as our resources grow. We've accomplished so much here in a relatively short but difficult time. I've put this map at your station. Please take a few minutes to familiarize yourself with it"

An interactive map appeared in front of each of them, and the room remained quiet as they studied. Mara was intrigued by the shops she hadn't noticed in the main complex area. Moving through the map, she saw the apartments and eventually found the cafes she had visited with Gracelyn and Krey. She saw a small store which was labeled a grocery store, but she could not yet find a larger one. She found the clothing store where she and Gracelyn picked out her outfits. One unit was labeled Garments, one called Meditation and one was Medical. The large Food Production unit was marked on one of the satellites.

Her thoughts were interrupted by Zoe. "We have been monitoring your interests based on your activities and what you read, but we would also like your input on the employment areas you may want to pursue. Think about the jobs you were introduced to on the *Superstes*. Which did you enjoy the most, or which would you like to learn more about? You'll find a very brief and very broad description of the work that we need which is currently available for your entry level."

At this point, she looked at each of them and gave a knowing smile.

"As you should imagine, this is only a brief overview of the work we've been doing here. Look over the list now, and I will meet with you individually to answer questions and discuss what may interest you. All of these jobs are much needed and important to our continued survival." Again, the room fell quiet while they read. As Mara perused the list, she recognized the jobs from her travel time.

<u>Construction</u>: Work includes sites in Gateway or the larger facility in Ridgeway as needed. Demonstrate or acquire knowledge of structural engineering, 3D printing, nano tubular builds, and clear metals.

<u>Food Production:</u> Demonstrate or acquire knowledge of edible plant growth. Monitor existing hydroponic gardens and food supplies. Develop and propagate new crops and proteins as needed. Assist Helpers with crop harvests. Enhance food production through laboratory study and modification. Acquire knowledge in 3D printed food.

Garment Production: Work may include designing, assembling, or testing clothing with imbedded technology. Perform basic maintenance for AI garment tools and machines; develop new fabrics and designs suitable for Cytar's climate and long voyage travel.

Maintenance: Work includes extensive use of Helpers in cleaning, maintaining and repairing all facilities. Work will level up to coordination with Technology in maintaining the Helper network and integrated building technology.

Mining and Manufacturing: Work includes mining and processing raw materials. Coordinate drone, Helper and human miners and manufacturers. Continue the development and monitoring of the industrial internet of equipment and its data. Acquire knowledge in manufacturing components used in all areas with an emphasis on resources needed in technology.

Medical Assistant: Observe medical data from personal device and garment monitoring and workplace readings. Treat injuries. Review medical records software as needed. Monitor synthetic blood production and supplies. Assist Helpers with any needed surgeries. Assist Helpers in medical laboratories.

Technology Assistant: Monitor and maintain Helper software, assist and monitor AI development, data storage, expanding communication networks. Demonstrate or acquire knowledge in software development and newly connected products.

When the decision was made, Mara sat with Zoe to explain her choice. She remembered all of the interesting introductory assignments on the voyage, but she kept coming back to the food production because of her fascination with hydroponic gardening.

Zoe encouraged her decision. "The Food team will be happy to have your help. Our food production here is challenging and seems stuck in the old ways. Maybe you can bring some innovation to the group. I'll be sending information about food production to your reader for you to study. You will report to the Food Production plant on Novusday at ten hundred."

"Excuse me, did you say Novusday?"

"Yes, on Novusday. Let's see... today is Friday, so you'll report in three days," Zoe stated in a tone which suggested that the interview was over.

Mara stood. "Thank you. I'll look forward to it."

"You're welcome. Stop and have a refreshment while you wait for your ground transport," Zoe suggested.

Mara bypassed the green drinks being offered, even though others seemed to be enjoying them. She was eager to see Krey and tell him about her work decision. She recognized their Gsport as it pulled up, and Krey jumped out to greet her as the door opened.

"Home," was all he directed the vehicle before he gave her a quick hello hug.

"How was your meeting?" he asked, keeping his arm around her shoulders.

She leaned against him, summarizing the information, before she told him of her choice.

"They all had their pros and cons, but I kept coming back to the food production. I really think I know so little about any of the fields, except for the little introduction I had when we were traveling here."

"Well, you'll be surprised at how much you know. Food production is an important field, especially in this erratic environment. We've struggled in the past to maintain a stable food supply that's both nutritious and supplies enough calories. Plus, you know that you don't have to stay in one field forever. You can always change jobs in the future if this doesn't suit you."

"I have another question for you. What is Novusday? That's when I report to work."

"Novusday is the first day of our week," he explained. "When Cytar's orbit and rotations were first measured at the early colonization, they realized the easiest way to divide time most evenly for a year's rotation was to keep the twelve months we were accustomed to, but that required eight days in a week. So, they added a new day—Novusday. Interestingly and thankfully, the daily rotation of our planet is very similar to Earth's, however we have a longer orbit around our light, and we have slightly less mass which has created somewhat less gravity. Our bodies seem to readily adjust to the gravity and oxygen levels here. Cytar's spin axis is also more vertical, so our day and night lengths are more constant throughout our year. We're continually monitoring our rotation and time, making sure it's constant and reliable. So far, the pattern is consistent from year to year, which is what we want."

"Did they keep the other days the same and in order?"

"Yes, in our language."

Something began gnawing at her thoughts, the troubling realization that she had no real concept of the passage of time and dates. Like many of her suspicious concerns, they could not be articulated well enough to find a solution and, temporarily admitting defeat, crawled back into the shadows of her mind. It only took a moment for another topic to race forward.

"That reminds me of another question," she said. "I saw some of the others' screen materials were in languages I couldn't read, yet I can understand everyone."

There was a pause before Krey answered.

"Our translating software is excellent. It can translate most languages instantaneously. That's why you can understand almost everyone here no matter the language they speak."

The crew on the transport was well aware that, whenever possible, defects in a traveler's DNA sequence were treated with the appropriate gene therapy once Candidates boarded the *Superstes* and entered their unconsciousness state. Any obsolete implanted chips were routinely replaced. New ones containing updated capabilities with the latest translators, plus health monitoring nanobots were implanted or injected before they woke up. Each of the monitoring capabilities would be unlocked as needed.

Learning from experience that too much information too soon was never good, Krey chose not to divulge any other details concerning the translation software, or any of the advanced routine health monitoring. This new question brought his overly serious mind to thoughts of how observant and inquisitive she seemed for her short awake time.

He guided the conversation to the sky, which displayed purple-toned clouds stretching like gnarled fingers overhead.

"Wind storm coming. We'll be getting home just in time," he observed, glad that any further questions could be postponed.

29

The following day, just as Krey, Mara and Rocket were finishing their run, Mara decided to bring up the idea which had been ruminating in her head.
"Remember how much I loved it when you took me to visit the little green outdoor area on the ship?"

"Of course. It was one of my favorite spots."

"I was wondering why we couldn't start one of those here on Cytar. Do you think that would be possible?" He almost laughed before he realized how serious she was.

"Wow, I don't think anyone has taken the time to think of anything that isn't for basic physical or mental survival."

"A green space or a park would certainly add to everyone's mental well-being. I don't mean right away, but I think it's worth considering for the future. Do you think it would be okay for me to do a little research on the possibilities of a little project?"

"I guess it wouldn't hurt. Why don't you wait until after you learn more in Food Production? Maybe then you'll be able to see if it's even feasible here with our dramatic temperature changes and slightly different oxygen levels. We do have an extensive seed bank. It's stored in Ridgeway, but all sites, plus the *Superstes*, have a vault with seeds for future use and for insurance against a catastrophic event."

She broke into a happy grin at the prospect of having a colorful space in the midst of a sparse drab land. She would bide her time until the most opportune time presented itself. They were almost to the house when her wrist comm signaled a call."

"Hello, Gracelyn, how are you?"

"Doing great. I just heard you were going to study about our food production, and I thought you might want to start at the results and work backwards. How about a little field trip to our grocery store?"

"Yes, I'd definitely like to see that, thanks. When do you want to go?"

"Let's meet right after lunch, say 1300?"

"Sounds good, I'll meet you outside then."

The Gsport was already waiting when they met near their house entrances.

"Gateway Complex, main entrance," Gracelyn directed as they got in. "So," she began, "you look as if you've settled in beautifully. I'm glad for you and especially glad when I see how happy Krey is. He can be too serious, so you've been good for him. He deserves his happiness; he's worked so hard for our colonies."

"He's so kind and caring." Mara hesitated and then went on. "But I can't explain how strange it is to have no memory of my past. Sometimes I feel as if my emotions are such a mess, changing from happy to confused to upset. And other times I feel like I'm almost ready to grasp the things I need to know or remember, but can't quite reach them. But then, when I'm with Krey, I think everything will be fine. And you and Bertie have always been so helpful. I really appreciate it."

"Don't ever hesitate to call or come over if you just want to talk or have questions about anything at all. I think you're doing amazingly well. Try not to worry. I know that's hard to do, but everything will work out as it's supposed to," Gracelyn said reassuringly as they arrived at their destination. They continued through the main walkway and turned into a short, but pleasant lane. Mara was not expecting such a little store tucked away in this narrow walkway. The sign over the door simply said Groceries in bright green letters. She and Gracelyn entered a room only lined with a few shelves along the side walls and a low, short aisle in the middle. She looked toward the back, wanting to find the larger section of groceries but saw only a wall with a door leading to an office or small storage room. She looked at Gracelyn questioningly.

"This is our food showroom, if you will," Gracelyn explained. "Almost all of our groceries are ordered from and delivered to home. Your kitchen keeps track of your grocery inventory, as well as the best use date. It automatically reorders items as needed unless it's told otherwise. People come to this store perhaps to pick up a last-minute item or to view or taste the difference between two similar types of fresh or prepared foods. The home orders go directly to where you will be working in Food Production, where they will be picked fresh or prepared and delivered occasionally by workers or Helpers, but most commonly by drones."

"Gracelyn!" A happy voice interrupted them. A man with Tanak's features and wearing the ubiquitous dark pants and solid colored shirt emerged from the back room. "I haven't seen you in too long. What can I get for you?"

"Hello, Tylore. It's so nice to see you. I've brought Mara, Krey's bond from the expedition, to see the store first hand. She'll be working in Food Production. Mara, this is Tylore, the expert on the food items here."

Before Mara could answer Tylore spoke up. "Welcome Mara. I'm so glad you're here and happy for Krey. Please look around, and I'm here if you have any questions, but you're in good hands with Gracelyn. And just let me know if either of you want to taste anything."

"Thank you, I'll just look around for a few minutes." Her eyes swiped from wall to wall, thinking that a few minutes would more than enough time. Tylore smiled and began turning his attention to a man who had just entered the store.

Mara walked slowly down the aisle and was astonished to see so few selections. She saw one or two small bags of each item displayed with their names and prices. Many of the fruit selections were represented only by digital images. There were several protein products, but only a few with names she recognized.

"We have the basic capacity to grow grains and foods for sustainable health and nutrition with our limited water supply," Gracelyn went on, "and I'm afraid if a product doesn't meet the standard, we can't yet allocate resources to produce it. You will be learning about growing and developing more products to keep us healthy in this environment. The good news is we've eliminated most diseases just through proper diet." She waited as she noticed Mara's concentration.

"I know it seems a little strange, but you'll get used to this, and it will all make more sense after you start working in Food Production," she added with a reassuring look. "I just wanted you to see some of the products you'll be working on and to know where this shop was located in case you wanted to visit on your own. When we go back, I'll show you how we order from the house, just in case you want to add something to your food cabinet."

Once home, Gracelyn reiterated that the cold and frozen cabinets were both tracking their food supply and automatically reordering as needed. The customer requested grocery ordering, although rarely used, was easy to learn, and, somehow, seemed quite familiar to Mara. Residents received groceries based on availability, nutrition and caloric needs, so choices were often limited. For her information and practice, Gracelyn showed Mara how to enter the virtual grocery store, choose a few items from the images and descriptions and order them to be delivered. The Helper with whom she was conversing lived up to its name by asking and answering questions and reserving the information for future use.

"How will I pay?" she asked when the order was complete.

Gracelyn thought about her answer and decided she could answer with just the needed information for now, hopefully helping her to assimilate quickly to her new world. She would explain it with a basic answer and omit mentioning the complete implant updates during her travel to Cytar. She preferred to have Krey inform her when he felt the time was right.

"All of our currency is digital, so as soon as you entered the store it recognized you and linked your house to Krey's and your account. Your order will automatically be debited from your account. It's very simple really."

Mara was suddenly struck with a déjà vu feeling of already having experienced this shopping and payment information, but quickly dismissed it.

"Okay, sounds easy, I don't think I'll have any problems with that. Thanks for all this help and for the eye-opening field trip. Do you have time to stay and have some tea?"

"Oh, thanks, but I should get back to my side of paradise," Gracelyn joked as she left.

Mara went to Krey's office and found him reading in the chair near the window. When he saw her, he put his reader down on the small table. She wore a pleased expression as she walked over and sat on his lap and was rewarded with his arms encircling her.

"I had an interesting outing with Gracelyn," she started and continued until he heard all the details of her new experience.

"I love hearing about things you see and learn here," he said when she had finished. "It's like I'm seeing them through your eyes and remembering when I experienced all this for the first time. Plus, I'm learning a couple new things myself. I don't think I've ever been inside the grocery store."

She gave him a quick kiss then, and he returned the affection until she gently pushed him back and stood up, giving him a flirty, impish look.

"To be continued," she said, "but right now I'm hungry, so your wife will go prepare a meal for us.

"What did you say?" he asked.

"I said, your wife will prepare a meal for us. Is that all right with you?"

"Yes, that sounds great," but he now had a pensive look.

As she turned to leave the room, her eye caught a new photo in a digital tray on Krey's desk. She walked over and picked it up. It was a picture of them at the appreciation dinner. They were dressed up, looking just off to the side and smiling, her arm linked with his. He walked over and was standing behind her, looking at the photo.

"I love that picture and the memories of that evening," he said, placing his hands on her shoulders.

"I didn't know anyone was taking pictures that night."

"It was taken when our names were announced."

"It was a very special night," she said as she put the frame back on his desk, the first image of them together, and looked at him meaningfully. "I'll always remember it, and I'm glad we have this photo memory."

During the night, they were awakened by another intense electrical storm. It brought ferocious distant thunder and brilliant lightning flashes causing the storm shutters to engage, but this time Mara was curled up with Krey by her side under a warm, soft duvet. It was a comfortable feeling, knowing they were safe inside, secure from the wrath of nature. Krey draped his arm over her, and she fell back asleep. She rarely remembered dreams, but when she awoke, she had a fleeting remembrance of one where she was running to a lake near a row of brick homes, when the scene bizarrely changed to being on a flight, but she didn't know the reason or the destination. When she awoke, she wanted to describe the dream to Krey, but the memory of it faded like a drop of milk in hot coffee and was soon out of her thoughts.

30

Mara climbed into the Gsport on her first day of work, filled with excitement and a bit of nervousness, and settled next to Krey. On the way to the Food Production satellite complex, he pointed out several rectangular areas which had a lighter hue than the surrounding ground.

"Those are some of our grain production fields which are sowed below ground just deep enough to attempt to protect the crop from our fierce wind storms. All of the crops have been genetically modified to be more drought tolerant. You can see by the color variation that some of the plots have protective covers which also generate some of the power for the indoor Food Production sites. The hope is that the winds travel over the top of the lower plantings," he explained.

"We also have several older open pit fields in a number of configurations, some with the protective dirt berms running horizontal, some vertical, or running both ways, as well as control fields grown above ground. Everything is still in the experimental stages. We're slowly trying to develop outdoor crops to supplement our hydroponic gardens."

"Are they satisfied with how it all works?" she wondered as she looked out at the grain fields, which resembled golden patches on a brown quilt of soil.

"For the most part, yes. If we're really blessed with some good weather, we sometimes get all the plots to produce a good crop. Depending on the ferocity of the storm, damage can still be incurred, and entire above-ground plantings can be obliterated in violent storms. We're trying to modify outdoor crops to be sturdier. I think you'll find your work very interesting. Everything is a work in progress here. I can tell you that those delicious breads that Gracelyn had for our homecoming were quite special and not commonly available. Each colony specializes in different grains. Ridgeway grows most of Cytar's oats, and Apogee has the rice."

Past the core Gateway center, the Food Production satellite emerged like building blocks which had been forgotten in a sandbox. Their vehicle passed one tunnel entrance and slowed to travel into a wider entrance before stopping in front of the middle set of double clear doors.

"I'll be at the Transport center, where we went the other day. Call me when you're finished, and we'll see if we can coordinate a ride home. If not, take a Gsport on your own. Now go get 'em." Krey gave her a supportive wink as she said goodbye.

A Helper greeted Mara and led her to a small reception area.

"Welcome. This is the area where you will report each day. I hope you have a productive day." The Helper smiled and left Mara waiting

Moments later, a door opened and a man entered with disheveled hair, graying at the temples. He was dressed in the most common black pants and a blue shirt, reminiscent of transport crew's uniforms. The clothes seemed a bit faded and worn, but this man looked as if he deemed his work a priority over the utilitarian nature of clothing.

"Welcome, Mara. I'm Larón, and I'm more or less in charge of the operations here. I can't tell you how happy I was when I heard you were interested in learning about this field. We can use the help, let me tell you." She immediately liked him. He had a kind but tired looking face, like he had been putting in too many long hours at work.

"I hope I can learn quickly and soon be of some help to you," she said as they entered a hall.

"This is my office," he pointed as they passed a room with a table and two chairs.

Mara caught sight of three large wall screens with information and diagrams on them.

"Feel free to drop in any time I'm here. We'll get you a tour of our facilities, which are not as large, or as advanced, as we need them to be. We expand when can, when we have the raw materials and the resources. Manufacturing is currently very busy with a couple of major projects, but we have our requests in and will eventually expand in stages."

He stopped at an open doorway and said, "I'm going to hand you off to Risha now. She will be your trainer and mentor. She's very knowledgeable and will get you started on good footing."

A gregarious woman with rich, dark skin, short, wavy hair and beautiful, smiling eyes greeted her.

Transport

"Hello, Mara, welcome aboard. I've got lots to show you today for an overview, and then later, we can narrow it down to what you'll be learning first. Sound like a good plan?" Her energy seemed contagious.

"Sounds good to me. I'm in your capable hands, so lead the way," Mara said enthusiastically.

They entered an elevator and descended a level, where a two-passenger cart was waiting. Risha drove them to their first stop, and Mara's enthusiasm quickly changed to astonishment. A large, cavernous facility stood before them, containing layered rows of tiered green plants growing in row upon row of enriched water. Overhead lights beamed down on a worker wearing a white lab coat and hat. Monitoring stations were spaced throughout the impressively sized room and drones were flying to read data. Modules were moving overhead with mechanical arms holding the "eyes" which were checking and harvesting mature plants.

"This is the main vegetable growing area for Gateway. We have other smaller rooms for important monocultures, most notably soybeans. We also have our starter room for seedling development. We monitor the growth and success rates of each species in relation to their nutrition. We have a central lab for this station to work on fertilizers, modifications in the environments and genetic modifications to improve production. We share all data with Apogee and Ridgeway.

"You'll be learning about the growing needs of all our food. Some need light to geminate, some darkness, some need a type of medium to support growth. You'll be checking and monitoring far-red and blue light and how we regulate them for maximum production. Luckily, our unique mineral-rich soil is perfect for many plants which need a medium to begin development. Whenever possible, we filter and recycle our precious water."

They traveled on through a narrow tunnel which opened to yet another surprise. Before them were four large aquarium tanks with various species of fish.

"This is our Aquaculture Station. We're very proud of the fact that we were able to successfully bring fish here, but producing and keeping them alive certainly keeps us on our toes. We're in the process of developing a more plant-based protein food for them, as it's too difficult to reproduce the total fish-based diets which sustained them in the wild. You'll soon learn that maintaining enough clean water and proper food for healthy fish is always a challenge."

Risha was pointing to the low cylinders near the tanks. "Those pumps keep the water continually aerated, and those pipes move dirty water to where it can be filtered to remove solid waste to be processed for fertilizer. Those control units monitor and maintain proper pH levels, temperature, water flow, etc. None of this is at as large a scale as we need, but right now our manufacturing unit is busy with another project, and finding enough good water remains our nemesis."

"I'm surprised at the size of the fish," Mara commented. "I was expecting much smaller varieties." The words were barely out of her mouth when she turned and saw a tank full of small sardines.

"The large fish represent generations of natural selection, breeding for size to produce more food for us. The sardine production can hopefully be increased because it could be an important source of fats for us." She pointed to Mara's right. "The block of narrow cylinders grows the plankton for the sardines. It's all too small and experimental now."

"How many people does this facility feed?" Mara asked.

"Gateway's population is currently just under 700. I think Ridgeway's population is a little more now, but Apogeeway is only around 550. That might not sound like many to feed, but growing anything here seems like an uphill battle, and any major problem could lead to near starvation. It's why we also have to keep some food reserves in case of an event catastrophe. The *Superstes* acts as an additional seed repository and mini food lab in the event of a catastrophic loss here."

"Do the other settlements also have facilities like this?"

"Ridgeway is the original colony, then came Gateway and lastly Apogee. Both are developing their own impressive food production capabilities, and we each specialize in a few crops depending on soil or water.

They drove on past a solid wall and stopped in front of a clear window overlooking a large area. As they peered in, Risha explained, "This is what I like to think of as our community's central kitchen. This is where we process and prepare ready-to-eat foods, or foods which need little preparation before consuming. This facility also prepares the food for all transport expeditions, plus there is also a bakery section which produces our limited breads. Behind that wall is our drink production area. We produce a soy-based drink which everyone calls milk in a nod to our former homes. Some containers of citrus flavored water are produced, but variety is not one of our strengths at the moment. We have a few innovative, independent individuals who produce limited amounts of coffee and tea. Maybe someday we can add that, but someday is a big word here. Because we can't support large animals, all of these foods must meet specific nutrition and caloric guidelines. All production is logged into the data center."

The place was alive with activity. There were long counters, conveyor belts moving products, and chutes bringing supplies from overhead tracts. A worker and a Helper were overseeing a section of an automated production line of preparing, scanning, packaging, and sorting packages to be sent to fulfill the day's orders. Other workers assisted in all areas, with drones moving in and out when prompted. Mara smiled when she recognized a Mopmop moving through the aisles.

They continued on, curving up and around until the next stop. "This is our small animal farm, and probably our least advanced venture, but sometimes there's only so much we can do now to produce healthy live animals; plus, this doesn't seem to be on the highest priority for resources. This facility is only partially below ground level. This allows us to open skylights and side ventilation as weather permits but also puts us at increased risk during storms," Risha continued.

"In general, the animals are produced to provide citizens with good meat protein for one or two meals a week, if that. We just don't have the grain production capacity yet to support a large meat production. Out of necessity most of our population is accustomed to a largely vegetarian diet."

She led the way to the middle of three rectangular buildings. "The building on your left houses rabbits, grown for protein, but as you'll learn, we waste nothing here, so we also harvest the fur pelts." Mara immediately thought of the warm fur collar on her long coat.

"The building on your right houses our pigeon aviaries. This middle one is the largest, and it is our chicken and egg ranch."

They entered a small entryway with a window.

"We won't go inside because we don't want to introduce any contaminants to the site. You can see that the robots that work here are an older model, but they work well for the tasks here until we can get more materials for bigger conveyors. They wear no covering which can hold or transfer germs, and they are docked each night in a disinfectant chamber. As you can see, everything is mostly automated, but in some ways it's still quite old fashioned because these are real animals with specific needs."
A four-legged robot laden with heavy grain sacks was moving through the building and stopped on the far side. It

shifted up to two legs, now using two appendages as arms to hoist feed into an automated feeder. Mara watched as metal funnels moved along troughs depositing feed while chickens wandered over and starting pecking. Several dozen of the feathered birds were wandering in large cages, eating their feed and drinking from narrow water tubes suspended from the top of the coops. Eggs were rolling to a collecting conduit as they watched. Mara was thinking about numbers and, although she could not determine the exact quantity of birds here, it could not possibly be enough to feed Gateway. No wonder most of their meals were vegetarian.

"We could use more chickens, but as I've mentioned, there's a fine balance between the numbers of animals we can maintain with the amount of feed we can produce for them. In a few weeks these chickens will be processed for their meat. The coops will be sterilized, and then a new crop of laying hens will be brought in. We also process the chicken litter for fertilizer."

Risha paused and looked at Mara, who had been quietly taking in all the new information.

"Now, I still want you to see one of our orchards and the grain fields, but let's save that for another day. Before your eyes totally glaze over, let's get back to the office area, have something to drink, and get you set up for some learning and working."

31

Krey was sitting at a smooth, clear surface tilted at a forty-five-degree angle. He was studying an open application, and two active air screens were glowing above him. He was just finishing some correspondence when he heard a two-tap knock. He looked up and was pleased to see Tanak standing in the doorway.

"Hey, there's the man!" Krey said with a big smile while changing the angle of his work surface to be parallel with the floor. "How's it going?"

"That's what I came to ask you. How's our special woman doing? You both looked like you were enjoying yourselves at the dinner."

"We were. It was a great evening, wasn't it? I think she's doing remarkably well considering all the adjustments being made in a short time. Gracelyn and Bertie were a Godsend those first couple of days."

"Well, I have to say, I think you look the happiest I've ever seen. Mara seems healthy? No concerns?"

Krey nodded, but his expression became more serious. "I'm very happy. Mara is well; she's actually starting a work session at Food Production today." His voice trailed off a bit.

"Do I detect an "if" or a "but" coming?" Tanak was studying Krey.

"No, not exactly. Maybe I'm just being overly sensitive because I care for her. No, not just care, I love her, Tanak, but she seems to be asking an awful lot of questions, which I don't remember other Candidates doing. And the other day she used the word wife when we were talking. I don't think she's heard that word with us, so it had to come from her memory."

"Hmm, interesting. I can see where that could concern you, but it's probably nothing. Anything else?"

Krey, hesitated, looked at Tanak, and said, "She knows. I almost ruined everything by letting her see the Cytar transport that ferried us here. She seemed to be adjusting so well and was so interested in everything; I wanted to share it with her. She became quite upset. Seemed she couldn't align all the information she was seeing with the memory blocks. I thought she was doing so well, but I think it was too much too soon. She asked about the *Superstes* and how far out it is. It won't be long before she'll want to see what it looks like and why we're here. I hope it doesn't trigger more issues before she's ready and her memory gradually comes back."

Tanak was quiet, looking thoughtful. Hearing no response, Krey continued, "And she often comments about her foggy memory, as if she can almost remember something but not quite get it. What will happen if it all comes back to her at once? Have you heard of any other snags like this?"

"Not that I know of, but I'll check the records and comments from all these new Candidates' accounts and see if there's any pattern. With that early wake-up, she might be unique to these issues. I'll get back to you; it's probably nothing to worry about."

"Thanks, Tanak. How are you doing? Everything okay?"

"Oh yeah, never a dull moment, but that's why we signed up for this. We don't like dull. But I am glad to be back for a while on solid ground and in some bigger spaces. It seems like it takes longer now to get acclimated to this place after a long trip." He shrugged and gave one of his wry smiles. "It's all good. Say hello to Mara for me, and I'll let you know if I find any anomalies in Candidate reports."

"Great. Thanks, and I'll give your regards to Mara. She thinks highly of you," Krey said lightly, but he was hoping no problems would be found.

He turned back to the inventory report of the supplies which were acquired on the expedition. The products had been coded as they were released from their sealed and sanitized quarantine pods and ferried in from the ship. It had been a very successful trip, both in terms of the quality and skills of Candidates and in the quantity of materials brought to Cytar. Looking over the list, he was amazed and very thankful for the procurement team's diligence and success in less than optimum conditions. They had to be very nearly magicians to obtain this massive number of supplies.

His eyes scanned the names of tools, medical equipment, electronic components and hardware, raw materials, seeds, packets of soil probiotics for experimentation with their near sterile ground, even an odd assortment of small machines, some for immediate use, and some to be used for parts. Helpers could begin to study and replicate or improve almost everything on the list. The advancement of the community capabilities was remarkable. Gone were the days when everything had to be brought on planet.

Through many years of hard work and sacrifices, Cytar had become basically self-sufficient, and he knew that all these supplies from the latest expedition would enhance that process and improve their quality of life. It was likely to be a very long time before another expedition would be undertaken, and it might not be back to Earth. It was strange to think about never going back, like cutting an umbilical cord to a lifeline. The finality of the thought struck deeply. He hoped they had made the right choices, and that they could gradually improve, and expand their knowledge and the communities.

The wish lists of items given to the procurement team were for very specific needs and products to supplement or free the workers here for other jobs. But everyone knew that some of the most prized items brought to the planet were often the most unusual and unnecessary for survival. A successful transport mission arrival was like Santa flying in on his sleigh. One year, the most coveted items were a few boxes of basic sporting equipment: a few basketballs, some baseballs, long since worn and tattered, and a nice variety of good liquor. When these items were gone, there would be no more in the foreseeable future. Peanut butter and denim jeans attracted attention and became the hottest items from another mission. Krey smiled. He still wore his Levis from back home. He wondered if there would be a surprise on this shipment.

He almost laughed out loud when he came to the section of consumables and saw some good-sized quantities of coffee and tea on the list, which some veritable wizard was able to acquire. Whoever secured these items should get a sorcerer's award. It would be difficult to bring enough pounds of either vacuum packed and deep-frozen product to satisfy these citizens. Every package would be in high demand and definitely bring a premium price.

His thoughts turned to the hobby growers here who had created some ingenious greenhouses to grow coffee and tea plants. The original plants were cultivated from beans and seeds which were successfully preserved or grown during voyage experiments. The local coffee roasting and tea processing was becoming quite successful, and the crops, although still limited, were gradually expanding into a nice little business. Too bad the beverages were not considered essential enough for Food Production to expend valuable resources for large scale production. They have had good success with hardy chicory, which was sometimes used to extend the coffee, but Krey could never get used to the flavor. *Better just keep that stuff for nutrition in salads.* Nothing was easy on this unforgiving planet, making every resource and effort focused on survival.

He sat back, thinking of what the first landings must have been like, when crude robots began building the first rudimentary structures while relaying habitat information back to the old space facilities. The time exchange between communications was horribly long. He could not imagine how difficult it must have been for the first settlers, leaving loved ones on one-way missions, living in small primitive pods while slowly building the infrastructure. So much sacrifice, so many accidents and deaths. There were the expeditions that set off and were never again heard from and, still now, knowing there was never a guarantee for success on any mission. This last thought gripped his heart in a painful grasp.

He purposely nudged his thoughts to Tanak. He wondered if Divine intervention hadn't played a part in meeting the Creos. How else could one fathom the chances of a desperate transport finding our ship in the vastness of space? Almost 300 souls were crammed on board in a last chance effort to leave their dying Creotarn in an attempt to save their species. Since that fortuitous event years ago, the two classes of humans have made great scientific strides by combining their knowledge.

Their procurement missions were only possible because they had been lucky enough to find traversable worm holes and gravitational waves which allowed travel to such incomprehensible distances in reasonable time frames. That, and the advances in energy and electromagnetic propulsion, which gave them the speed they needed. No, he reprimanded himself; all this was not luck, more like unparalleled hard work and great minds, and Lor's uncanny abilities at the helm, with the assisted brain that was able to figure out equations needed for locating pathways with good reliability. As captain, he had been meeting with scientists who had found actual structure and symmetry in the solar systems. Maybe that's how he was finding the reliable travel vectors with the help of his AI syncing. But even with all their knowledge, Krey knew there was still no absolute assurance they could find a path to return to their original destination.

His mind continued to meander down the often-traveled lane of wonderings and observations, paved with speculation and uncertainty. Mankind is an enigma. At its best, reaching for lofty goals, determined to survive, seeking love and kindness; at its worst, being destructive, power hungry, petty and cruel. He shook his head to rid himself of his brooding, thoughtful mood, one no doubt exacerbated by the recent return from a long voyage. Better not to think so much, stay positive and be grateful for all they've accomplished. His thoughts turned to Mara. Here they were, dealing with vast difficulties, but in the end, it all seemed to revolve around love.

Forcing himself to return to his work, he monitored the supply requests and began delegating materials to the proper stations, before setting the transfers in progress. They could not afford to have anything lost or misplaced. He was eager to finish for the day and be home with his wife. He smiled, pleased that Mara had used that word.

When he decided he couldn't concentrate any longer, he checked and saw that Mara was already home. He arrived to find the lights on and tail wagging Rocket at the door, a pleasant change from coming into an empty house. He heard dish sounds from the dining area and found Mara at the all-cook.

"How did your first day go?" he asked when he saw her. "I kept thinking about you and everything you're going to learn."

She needed no further coaxing to share her day. "It was quite overwhelming, and we just skimmed the top of facilities and functions. My mentor is Risha, and she's awesome, and I have so much to learn from her," she said as she proceeded to rattle off all she saw, barely stopping for a breath.

Her voice was animated with excitement as she spoke, and her face was flushed with the stimulation of all she had learned. He listened and watched admiringly, noticing how nice she looked when she glanced up, with her hair pulled back and casually tied at the nape of her neck.

When they brought their dinner to the table, they exchanged more news of their day as they ate. Krey eventually told of Tanak's visit, but never mentioned the conversation which concerned her.

32

The first Food Production work week progressed quickly. There was a steep learning curve to digest all of the information presented, and Mara made the normal mistakes of a new worker. Risha was patient and had organized the work in a logical order to facilitate her understanding. Mara often recorded notes on the new material to review later. She would come home and share her day with Krey before reviewing more information on her reader.

If she was currently impressed with the indoor food production facilities, she was astonished when Risha showed her the small but fruit laden orchards, most grown below level as if in a pit, with flat power producing movable panels above the sunken areas. The protective panels closed at dusk or during storms and opened at first light. The trees were much smaller than Mara had imagined, and she was surprised at their production levels. Most trees were grafted to grow more than one type of fruit. Citrus trees grew oranges, lemons and limes. There were also trees growing various types of stone fruit and those with multiple varieties of apples.

"We're using some old methods here with the grafting. You can see we've genetically altered these plants to grow bigger and more abundant fruit on smaller trees. We're willing to try all kinds of techniques to produce our less than optimum amounts of fresh food," Risha had explained. "So far, our variety is limited, but our hope is to expand. We have a separate important orchard for olive trees and an experimental palm tree area to produce our oils. We've had trouble hybridizing both trees to withstand cold nights, even in protected plots. Little by little, we're making progress, but all of this is a big experiment, and we only hope we don't lose too many plants in the process."

Their most prized possessions were the bee hives which were located in their own protected areas near the orchards. The bees were important for their pollinating efforts, but the real prize was the bees' honey, the colonies' only sweetener. A small crop of sugar beets was being maintained in anticipation of future expansion for an additional sugar source. Mara was amazed at seeing the unexpected viable bee colony, but Risha had another surprise when she pointed to a tall, narrow cabinet near the hives.

"That cabinet is the charging station for our bee bots." She opened a door revealing a wall of beelike mini drones, fully charged and waiting. "We use these auxiliary pollinators to help our limited bee population. The bots are quite effective and ensure that our crops will be pollinated in a timely manner. We have to have alternative pollinators in the event of a hive collapse."

If possible, the grain fields were even more impressive, most now planted below level, many with similar coverings as the orchards. Each field was planted with enough spaces between rows for autonomous equipment to plant, monitor, irrigate or harvest the crops. Risha told of a nearby underground mill, and she promised that tour when they had more time.

The following morning, when Mara exited the Gsport at Food Production, Krey gave a nonchalant, "Have a great day," but his face revealed a handsomely sly grin before he added, "Oh, by the way, Gracelyn, Bertie and I arranged a little surprise for you."

Her job seemed to be channeled into lab work, so she couldn't think of what type of surprise could come of that. When she entered the lab, Risha was already busy looking at comparison data from the hydroponic stations.

"Good morning, Mara. I'm going to be working with Larón for a few days. It sounds like we need to visit Apogeeway, so I'm going to send over a Helper for you to work with."

"Okay, is everything all right there?"

"I hope so," Risha answered.

"They've asked us to look over some projects, and we're taking a few requested supplies over as long as we're going. You can call or message me if you have any questions while we're gone."

She finished up just as her wrist comm announced the waiting transport to Apogeeway, leaving Mara to work alone. The morning progressed normally until a familiar voice said, "Good morning, Mara."

She turned around and was elated to see Cali standing in the doorway.

"Cali! Hello! What are you doing here?"

"I am your Helper. I have recently been updated with current knowledge of food production and am here to work with you."

"This is a wonderful surprise! I'm happy to see you!" Mara said, feeling as if she had been reunited with an old friend. In a strange way, she was comforted by having her non-human known entity in this unknown world, with all of its many new discoveries. She was happy to be with familiar, efficient Cali and even welcomed her terse speech.

Cali gave her usual smile, "Thank you. I am here to assist you. Please give me my assignment."

Mara was so new to the work; she barely knew what to say. She finally managed to explain that she was looking at production yields and genetically modifying corn plants to determine what, if any, changes needed to be made. They were working to create smaller plants which produced larger amounts of the corn kernels.

Cali rapidly began displaying data in front of her, and from then on, the two were a team. Mara was amazed at Cali's programming and made a note to compliment Gracelyn and Bertie on their work. She was watching her Helper work, recalling a conversation she had with Krey about the capabilities of their artificial intelligence.

"We are trying to learn from others' mistakes," he had told her, by not making Helpers too self-aware and capable of programming themselves. "We don't want them developed to the point they don't need us. That would defeat the purpose of all our sacrifices to continue our species."

What a frightening and delicate balance, she thought, but she readily welcomed the assistance her Helper was providing.

33

Cali's ancillary knowledge made the work progress smoothly and quickly. Mara returned home before Krey and, feeling less mentally exhausted, decided to take Rocket for a run. She had learned a route which took her over more even ground, first wandering through the five other houses and then onto the open spaces, eventually looping back to their home. Today, as she passed the last house, she heard a woman's voice shout, "Rocket!"

Mara slowed and stopped when she saw Rocket run toward the woman.

"Hi neighbor, you must be Mara," she said as she gave attention to Rocket. "I'm Roz. My husband, Denin, and I live here, and I've seen you out with Rocket but never could catch you to say hi." She was smiling and wisps of blond hair were escaping from a knit cap.

"Hi, yes, I'm Mara, nice to meet you. You're the first I've met or even seen in these houses. How do you know Rocket?"

"Oh, a lot of people know Rocket because he's so rare. There are only a handful of real dogs here. Our food supply can't really support pets, but a few years ago some puppies survived on a transport, brought on as stowaways, I'm sure, and Rocket was one of them. We have some AI pets here, although most are reserved for long journey expeditions or special assignments. Do you mind if I join you on your walk or jog?"

"Not at all. I'd welcome the company," Mara answered cheerfully as they started off.

Roz named the people who lived in the nearby houses and where they worked, but the names and places flowed too quickly to all be remembered on the first telling. She explained that she worked in Maintenance and had learned from Gracelyn that Krey had entered a life pledge ceremony while on the expedition.

"News travels fast in our little community, and I won't lie," Roz laughed, "I was curious to meet the woman who captured Krey's attention. There are probably some disappointed women in Gateway."

"He's a pretty special man, all right," was all Mara wanted to share, but she was thinking about his patience with her, about the tender love and the passionate love, and it all made her feel happy to be alive in the moment. Still, she decided, she didn't know Roz enough to talk about Krey or confide any of her personal feelings, so she changed the subject.

"How many transports are out now?" she asked.

"None now," Roz said. "I heard the last shipment of supplies has been ferried in from the *Superstes*, which is our only long voyage expedition ship now. There is one small shuttle transport that stays with her, but the others are here. I'm sure you've heard from Krey that the ship before yours, the *Navigator*, has never been heard from and is assumed lost with 41 souls and 19 Helpers aboard, plus two shuttles. It's been a terrible loss to us, and I don't think any of us have fully recovered emotionally. It was a great relief to have everyone return safely, and we're very thankful to have 55 new citizens here."

Mara only remembered Tanak mentioning that ship at the appreciation dinner, never realizing the immense tragedy surrounding it. They were jogging back close to the houses, but she was still thinking of the terrible loss of lives and equipment, and the impact it would have on such a small community in a remote world. It was the first she had heard of the total number of Candidates who had arrived with her. They had continued on Mara's usual route, talking while they ran at a comfortable pace, and eventually circled back to Roz' house. They jogged in place while they said goodbyes and made plans to meet again soon.

The tragic news of the lost *Navigator* lingered in Mara's mind as she contemplated the fragility of life, especially in this singular world, and how perilous the journey here must have been. She was still thinking of how alone she would be in this new realm without Krey, and for the first time she truly acknowledged the deep feelings she now had for him. She was still in her reflective mood when he arrived home. She immediately went to him with a needy embrace and loving kiss which he returned.

"Is something wrong?" he asked when he saw her pensive expression.

"I met a neighbor, Roz, and she told me about the loss of the *Navigator* and the all the people that have never again been heard from. It's really affected me in a more profound way than I was prepared for." She looked to him for reassurance, but his face looked stricken and his body went rigid.

"What is it? What's wrong?"

It took a moment before he spoke. "My older brother was aboard that ship."

34

Mara felt gut punched. "Oh, my God, I'm so sorry; you never said anything. I didn't know you had a brother." All the unknowns in her life came reeling around her. "I don't know anything about your family. We don't know enough about each other. Come and sit and talk to me."

She took his hand and led him to the little sitting room, which became the quiet space for Krey to talk and Mara to listen.

As soon as they sat on the sofa, she said, "tell me about your brother and your family. I can't remember mine, so this is important for both of us."

Krey just sat still, looking at the blank wall in front of them. Unable to produce comforting words, she held his hand and waited quietly, hoping he could share his thoughts.

In a low monotone, he began. "I idolized my brother, Reyver. He was two years older than me, smart, good looking, always took care of me, and I wanted him to be proud of me. When he decided to come here, I knew I wanted to follow him. We arrived here together ten years ago. I was young, didn't know much, but I was eager to learn and, like Reyver, determined to make this community work. He guided me, taught me, advised me. We worked so hard, but we had a great time, and we felt like we were really contributing to this project.

"When they decided to send transports out again for reconnaissance and supply runs, Reyver and I were two of the first to volunteer. We both had a successful trip on the *Superstes* a few years before, and the *Navigator* was next to deploy. It was an older ship, but had been updated and retrofitted regularly. We both signed up again to go together. He was chosen, and I was assigned to the *Superstes*, which was to leave on another supply run a year later."

His voice was filled with pain as he continued. "All the limited communications from the *Navigator* were normal before we left. We knew there would be virtually little or no contact with them once we were in space.

"By all standards, our expedition was considered a great success. For me, the most important aspect of the whole trip was meeting you. When we returned, I couldn't wait to see my brother and exchange travel stories, learn more from him, and I wanted him to meet you."

He sighed here, still looking at the wall. "They decided not to tell us until we got home. They had lost all communication with his ship. Decided it would be too detrimental to our crew and passengers. And it would have been. Nothing we could have done. I suspected a problem when we heard no news of their contact with Mars, but the mind sometimes refuses to acknowledge painful outcomes. You, with your positive, inquisitive personality, were the one who kept me focused and staying in the moment on that journey.

"To this day, we've never heard from that ship, and it is considered lost. Just before our flight returned, there was communal funeral service for all on board, and a tribute was erected in Ridgeway, where most of the crew were from. I visited shortly after we returned. That was the night I got home so late and found you asleep in my office." He stopped, and Mara noticed that tears had welled up in his eyes.

After a while, she said, "tell me about your parents. Do you have other siblings? How did they feel about you both leaving?"

"No, it was just Reyver and me. My parents still live in the same housing where we grew up. My dad and mom are both in the space program, in the satellite division. Everyone in the program understood all the hardships in deep space travel, sometimes especially for those staying behind. They never discouraged us; they felt there could be a better future for us in a new place."

He stopped talking, and Mara was thinking of more questions when he continued, "I had only a brief time to talk to them, hopefully, for their sake, on a hidden platform. I had to tell them the little I knew about Reyver. I think they suspected a problem, having not heard from him or any news in so long. But, in the end, they said they were still glad we left. It was doubly hard, because I'm sure we'll never go back, so I'll never get to communicate with them again. It was a tough goodbye."

Her light-heartedness had evaporated. *This place makes you serious, robs you of the ability to be carefree. There's a reason for his thoughtful personality.*

He looked at her and gave a weak smile. "I'm glad I told you about Reyver. I never have been able to talk about him, but it's not good to try and bury the painful feelings of loss."

"We're just getting to know each other, really," she said. "It's going to be important for us to talk and share information and feelings. I'm sorry I don't have much to share with you. I wish I could remember my family."

They sat quietly for a few more minutes, until Krey pushed his shoulders back as if gathering strength. Having purposely thrown off his sadness, he turned and looked at her with his normally assured, solid countenance.

"I have faith that someday you will," he answered as they got up and headed into the dining area.

35

Mara soon realized that every person in this thinly populated world had been, in some way, personally affected by the loss of the *Navigator*. The respect for their forbearance only grew, as she observed their unwavering commitment to improve life on Cytar.

A tranquil time had settled on the communities with the sweet comfort of routines. The busy days passed as days always do with home and work blending and flowing together to become life. The only tedious days were the ones when tenacious night winds decided to persevere throughout the day, causing everyone to remain indoors. Tasks were saved especially for those days when no one wanted to venture out in the cold, dirty air turned brown by blowing soil. Thankfully, those days were not the norm and, for several weeks, life continued with exceptional efficiency, and work efforts at the stations were all showing good progress.

In former eras this would have been the time when extraneous group activities would have blossomed. On Cytar, the inherent human need for constant face to face social interaction had diminished over the years. Perhaps it was the unique environment, or the massive energy needed to ensure survival, or the increase in cyber communications and activities, combined with the mundane lack of larger group facilities. The human socialization need became balanced with the immense workloads in the emerging communities. During private time, community members became satisfied with home activities, the occasional dinner with friends, the interactive virtual and hybrid game competitions or occasional informal outdoor sporting get-togethers when weather permitted. Mara continued going for walks or a run, alone, with Krey or with her new friend, Roz, who proved to be very smart, quick witted and entertaining.

Krey introduced Mara to a few of his home games, some older and newer virtual games in their limited metaverse, and she was trying, without complete success, to become a worthy opponent. Somehow, it was the challenge and not the outcome, which created the intrigue for her. They played in the sitting room where the holograms created new virtual worlds of adventurous entertainment, and her favorite game soon became *Skyrider*. She loved to compete and race flying transports to supply stations without crashing, losing fuel capacity, or being captured.

He took the game more seriously, but she just loved the engaging competition, often without a care of the results. Her frenzied technique often involved shouting when in precarious situations, before collapsing in uncontrollable laughter after a total disaster. He loved teaching and watching her, and her joyfulness was frequently contagious. Here they were, like oil and vinegar, a perfectly balanced mixture, with just the precise blend of salt and pepper to create this rich, spicy mixture of his driven seriousness and her light hearted intelligence.

There were rare instances when time, weather and circumstances cooperated, allowing Krey and Mara to join others in their little neighborhood for some type of outdoor, spur-of-the-moment sport, usually their strange version of sandlot baseball. An old piece of clothing tightly rolled around some discarded material became a ball, and a piece of scrap metal was transformed into a bat, creating the peculiar juxtaposition of a historic amusement in a technically advanced world. Any outdoor group time was usually short and very infrequent, with too many life sustaining matters always pressing upon their survival energies.

On one very extraordinary occasion, however, a first live concert on Cytar was announced. The venue would be at the same Gateway Hall which hosted the appreciation dinner, and the only venue largest enough to hold a relatively adequate number of attendees. The concert was to be streamed to homes in Ridgeway and Apogeeway. Krey wondered if would have attended in person when he was single, but he saw Mara's interest, and it pleased him to accompany her. She wore her short black dress, he his dressier pants and shirt in honor of the extraordinary event it was.

She recognized the same musicians from the dinner, who played a medley of songs along with several others who showcased their newly learned skills. A few diligent and inspired people had made a drum set and accompanied some pieces. A small choir sang a variety of songs, some haunting and sad, some lively. The whole affair had an old-world charm, and it was a promising start to something that, heretofore, would not have even been dreamed of in this remote world. It was not the talent, but the fact that it had happened, a true cornerstone marking their graduation from survival to thriving, which heralded the triumph of their existence on the planet.

Often, during a period of such calm, the brain can be relieved of its energies spent solely on survival and can venture into more creative thought. It was then that Mara's notion for a park with bright green plants, that long dormant seed of an idea, found fertile ground. It grew, sending powerful thought tendrils, insisting, demanding that it be heard.

Krey's support gave the encouragement to give voice to her plan. Risha, with her optimistic, can-do demeanor, was the first to be entrusted with the idea. The wish for creating a green sanctuary similar to the one she had seen on the ship was presented to her one morning at work. Mara told of wanting to start with a small outdoor space for study and experimentation with plants in this unique climate, in the hopes of eventually creating a green park. She would need the use of the lab, helpers, and seeds.

"Wow," was Risha's first exclamation. "How did you ever get to see that place on the *Superstes*?" And then without a breath, she answered her own question. "Of course, Krey took you."

Mara waited for some affirmation, her mind flashing

simultaneously between thinking she had revealed either the most ridiculous idea or the next best thing for Cytar. Risha was thinking about possibilities before she spoke.

"Well, Gateway has a fairly extensive seed vault here at Food Production. You'll have to run this by Larón and see what he thinks. I know people would enjoy it. The green space would be good for everyone's psyche, but it won't be easy, and I can't even imagine how long it would take to develop. But I think you should go for it anyway and ask Larón."

It took three attempts before Mara found Larón in his office listening to his reader. A tentative knock drew his attention.

"Mara, come in. How can I help you?"

"I'm here with a wild idea, which I hope you'll find as intriguing as I do.

He turned in his chair, now fully facing her. "I'm always interested in wild and intriguing ideas. Go on, please."

She had rehearsed the persuasive speech in her head, and her passion for the idea allowed her to easily retrieve her thoughts. She explained the benefits of a green park-like area and wanted his insight on the possibilities of developing a small test plot.

His eyes widened as her heard her suggestions. "Well, this is intriguing. I'm afraid we're always so focused on planting for food and nutrition we've never thought about the mental health which could be derived from plants. It's doubtful any plants from our seed bank could survive outside in this climate." He saw the disappointment on her face.

"Why don't you let me think about this and talk to some of my other Food Production colleagues and see about the capacity of our three food banks. It would require many hours of research and genetic modifications for this to have any degree of success. And it would have to be done in addition to some projects I need you to work on."

Her face brightened. "Oh, I understand that. I was just wondering if I could do some plant research and have access to some seeds, if anything looks promising."

"Well, it certainly would be wonderful if it were feasible. Let me talk to some of my people and get back to you. Give me some time while I check on some things myself and talk to the others, but I will eventually get back to you."

Mara left, happy that her idea was heard and knowing she would continue to cultivate its growth. She understood her tenacious nature well enough to know that once a thought gripped her mind, it would persist and never rest until it received her attention. In the meantime, she would do her work, enjoy her life and wait for word from Larón.

Sometimes life has other ideas.

36

It was as if Cytar had been domesticated. The land and weather were behaving. The meager plant life seemed to finally be proliferating. Work station production in all areas flourished with only the normal problems, which eventually could be solved. Krey had discovered happiness. He was still driven to help expand a sustainable community, but now he had a partner with which to share his life. He and Mara were working hard, enjoying each other's company as they learned more about one another while making a new life together.

And then, as if they should have been attuned to the foreshadowing, on one perfectly normal, calm day when the light rose with a particularly glorious brilliance, Krey, Mara, Gracelyn and Bertie were unexpectedly reminded that nature seems to abhor routines. They had just finished an enjoyable lunch together when all four of their wrist comms sounded simultaneous alarms, and all complacent contentment vaporized.

"Severe electrical storm warning with high winds," was the audible announcement piercing their complacency. "Event horizon in Gateway 47 minutes, Ridgeway 53 minutes, Apogeeway 58 minutes. Seek underground shelter. Wind monitor at Stellar Crest failed at 219mph sustained." The announcement began to repeat, but Gracelyn, Bertie and Krey were already on their feet. Mara's concern increased when she saw the distress on their faces.

"What's going on? What event horizon?"

Krey answered, "We don't have much time before there'll be no chance to react. We'll need to get any necessities for overnight and all meet in the walkway."

He looked at Bertie, "We'll take Rocket with us, but first I want to check outside."

"We know what to do; come on Gracelyn."

They were out the door without another word. Krey, with Mara following, went immediately outside and up in the yard in an effort to detect the storm front. Mara was looking toward the Gateway Complex, a peaceful scene washed in a clear light. She turned around to the alarming sight of a distant, yet enormous solid wall of ominous churning gray which began at the ground and rose immeasurably high, falling forward upon itself, moving, undulating toward them. The most frightening aspect was that it seemed alive and purposefully targeting them, rolling, advancing like an enraged demon with flashing lightning in its bowels.

Krey didn't linger, but quickly detoured to carry the patio settee into the enclosed walkway. Mara grabbed the outdoor chair and followed him. They went back out one last time while Krey made sure the gate to Rocket's kennel was secure before he took her hand and hurried inside.

"Go get anything you need--be quick," he said. He was waiting when she returned from their room, and ushered her into the enclosed walkway between the houses.

The nearby outdoor scene still remained deceptively tranquil. Not waiting for the automated severe weather response, Krey spoke to his wrist comm, "Engage all storm shutters." The bright walkway began to dim as a closure descended and covered the clear material. Gracelyn and Bertie had come from their house with Rocket, who seemed to sense the tension in the abnormal movements.

"May God protect us all," Gracelyn said as she and Bertie disappeared behind a door on the side of their house.

Krey opened a door on their side of the walkway and a light illuminated a downward stairwell. Rocket, not wanting to be left behind, hurried down followed by his owners. The stairs led to a small complete studio apartment.

"I never knew this was here," Mara said as she looked over the room with a bed, chair and a short counter with a small built in cooking appliance. The compactness of it all was reminiscent of her days on the transport.

"All buildings have complete underground shelters. They act as shelter from life threatening storms or any possible attacks."

"Attacks from whom? Are we in danger from attacks?" *What else could happen here?*

"Not that I've ever heard, but there are so many unknowns out there. We have deep space surveillance monitors in place which have never picked up any problems or contacts. These shelters are precautionary, mostly intended for weather events like this."

They settled in and checked for any news updates on their readers. It was quiet except for the hum of the air filtration until an explosive sound tore through the peace.

The overhead lighting went off, immediately followed by the illumination of two dimmer wall bars, giving the space a more unsettling ambiance.

"It's here," was all Krey said.

They could hear an angry persistent wind screaming overhead, interrupted by enraged electrical blasts ripping the air. The wind spared no bit of ground, uncontrolled and venting its power without letup. Not knowing the damage occurring above was the most unsettling element of waiting. The constant thrashing of the wind and violent thunder shocks wore on the nerves. Occasionally, a sharp unexpected thud would sound as if something had forcefully hit their side of the building, causing a startled lurch in Mara. Rocket sat nervously in a corner, receiving absent-minded pats from Krey.

The most disturbing sounds came when the winds built to shrieking blasts, imitating a rabid animal ready to devour their home. Mara tried not to envision the damage which must be occurring above them. She sat, she paced in the tiny space, and at some point Krey offered her a nutrition bar, but hunger evaded her. There was nothing to do but wait amidst the noise of the frightful storm, drifting in and out of sporadic sleep with the winds howling above. When Mara awoke, Krey was looking at the wall screen with a serious expression.

"What's happening?" she asked. The wailing wind sounds were gone, but now she heard muffled pounding sounds as if someone were peppering the walkway roof with small dense projectiles.

"The storm is passing," Krey said. "It's been raining hard for the last hour or so, very unusual here. We can use the water, but I hope this is over soon."

Over the next two hours, the rain sounds softened until the quiet hum of air flow could again be heard, and the brighter room lights returned. When their wrist comms announced an "all clear" message, they ventured out and met Gracelyn and Bertie emerging at the same time. The walkway shutters attempted to rise, but encountered damage half way up and stopped with an uneven tilt. They all stooped under to walk outdoors to a soggy, muted day.

The eerie calmness revealed a sullen sky and a storm damaged vista. Water from the torrential rain was still dripping and draining into any low spots and forming odd shaped puddles. It flowed down the slope to the clear door of the house, until it met the ground level drainage openings which channeled the water to underground cisterns.

The yard presented a dystopian landscape of an odd mixture of barren sticks and stems and mangled leaves, but the dwarf, thick-trunked trees remained, their heavy gnarled bark still intact, although the few remaining branches had been given a windward shave. The sturdy fence delineating Rocket's kennel was leaning in waves. Small broken branches were entwined in the decorative metal. The shade roof was nowhere to be seen, although a tiny piece still dangled from a corner of the fence.

They looked back at the house to discover that all of the exterior shutters facing the storm front were still in place but were damaged and unable to retract. The strong, long, sloped side of the roof covered with durable power cells looked at first glance to be largely spared, no doubt with the help of its imbedded protective metal grid. Artistically formed dunes of soil rested against the windward side of the house. Small, weak shadows appeared along wavy ripples in the mounds of wind driven dirt.

No one spoke while walking around, each was thinking of any yet unknown destruction and its consequences. They saw other neighbors out inspecting their homes, all of which seemed, with cursory inspections, to incur only minor problems. All gave quiet waves as if to reassure one another, but no one felt like visiting.

Bertie was the first to speak. "Food Production will have suffered the most damage."

Krey agreed. "We all may have to help there with clean up and plantings."

They returned indoors to a gloomy house with one side darkened by the dysfunctional shutters. Mara engaged the lights while Krey checked in to the Gateway headquarters. He spent a few minutes communicating with several stations before he talked to Mara.

"We're to work here today to repair and clean up what we can. We're near the top of the queue to have workers or Helpers come over to repair or replace shutters and inspect the roof." He noticed her somber expression. "Everything will be fine. We should get something to eat before we check the rest of the house and get to work."

The house power had been automatically turned off during the storm and immediately restored afterwards. A prepared meal was hastily heated and eaten without much conversation before the rest of the house was inspected. Mara was impressed by the integrity of the construction which withstood the wind blasts with the help of the heavy-duty shutters.

Outdoors was another matter. The windward side of the house would need some resurfacing, but no projectiles had penetrated the walls, perhaps the one benefit of scanty foliage unable to produce large damaging storm missiles. The four began moving windswept dirt dunes in the early afternoon and worked until dusk.

The fierce wind velocity blew most debris on whirling journeys far from their origins. The left-behind broken branches and tattered leaves were collected; soil was hauled from the rippled sandbanks against the house. The soggy dirt was redistributed as evenly as possible throughout the yard with care given not to disturb the pathetic remaining plant stubs. Most of the water pools were beginning to seep into the porous ground.

When tired muscles and the cold signaled a halt, they retreated inside for a late dinner together, before agreeing to meet in the morning to work at the Food Production station.

37

The morning landscape views on the way to the work satellite were disheartening. Gone were the scarce low shrubs and grasses, leaving in their place a few defiant sticks and bits of smashed grass blades whose deep tap roots refused to yield to the tempest. The former perfectly circular water collection basins were now irregular lakes whose edges were already showing the wet rings of soil absorption. "Will this ever recover?" Mara wondered.

Bertie answered, "The wet dirt will help for now, and if we could get plenty of light and some nice steady daytime rains the recovery will be faster, but this is setback for sure, and the day rains are rare and night measurable moisture is nearly nonexistent."

The grounds around the Food Production area offered no solace. All of the above ground control plantings were destroyed, leaving broken tree stumps in the orchards, and grain fields looking as if they had been mowed to the ground. The below-ground, uncovered, pit plantings fared only slightly better. The orchards had broken, twisted branches, but less total destruction, and a small amount of the fruit, although damaged, could be salvaged in the corners or lee edges of the pits. The below ground grain fields also suffered major damage, with the only consolation being in the fact that a fraction of the plants survived. The current situation was so dire that even the poor survival rate was actually considered a meager success. All of the excavated planting areas had filled, to some degree, with the blown storm soil, which would have to be removed.

Several citizens had shown up to help or for the needed moral support. Krey recognized Lor's daughter with a friend before noticing Kerry, and wondered if he personally looked as distraught as this budding coffee entrepreneur.

"Kerry, I'm surprised to see you here. I thought you'd be busy with the coffee plants."

"You mean what's left of them." Kerry's face reflected his worry and distress. "We lost so much. That's why I'm here, to see if there's an extra Helper that I can use tomorrow; but looking around, I'm guessing they'll all be spoken for."

"Were you able to save anything?"

"Oh, I have my original fully protected stock, but there's not much left of the field we had semi-outdoors. It's just discouraging. I'm just lucky I kept some plants in my storm shelter with grow lights in case something like this happened. It took so long to get to where we could sell a little and meet the needs of some people, and now it'll be almost like starting over." He sounded defeated, and Krey searched for some consoling words.

"It won't take quite as long this time, because of all your experience, and you have some of the infrastructure. You know all of us coffee fanatics will help in any way we can."

"Thanks, Krey. I'll have to catch up with you later." Kerry attempted a weak smile and was already wandering off toward the building entrance.

The gloves, shovels and rakes came out, and the people began to assist Helpers in removing branches, soil and debris from pits or against the low buildings. The broken remains were loaded into open vehicles and taken to shredders. Many of the damaged plants had simply disappeared and had most likely blown far out of sight. Late in the afternoon, Krey summoned Mara to join him inside the main work station. Larón and Risha were updating the reports from various sites.

Larón, in clothes looking more rumpled than usual, was rubbing his forehead as if he could make the worry lines disappear. He shook his head, took a deep breath and sighed.

"Sometimes I wonder if it wouldn't be better to just focus our energies on artificial food. I know that's not good for long term health, but this is discouraging." He sighed again in resignation and then visibly tried to project a better mood.

"The good news is we have no reports of casualties or major structural damage. We learn from each major weather event and our knowledge is paying off. The covered orchards and grains survived with non-catastrophic losses, meaning many of the plants survived, but the crop yield is greatly affected. The bad news is we've lost some major food products which will take time to reproduce. We did have at least one grain cover fail with disastrous results, and as you know, the unprotected fields and orchards are all but gone."

"What about the indoor plant and animal stations?" Mara asked.

"Power had to be cut to the hydroponic station," Risha began. "We're hoping that it was started again in enough time to limit damage. The freezing temperature warnings did not go off in that section, so we're optimistic. Many of the small animals survived, but a portion of the covers on the chicken and pigeon facilities were badly damaged, and all of the survivors seem quite agitated from the darkness and storm noise. Many are not eating or acting normally. The chickens' laying cycle is off, temporarily, I'm hoping. We tried to keep power going, although somewhat intermittently, for the Aquaculture center, and we're hoping the tanks were aerated enough to limit any losses there. We'll know more in the next 24 hours or so, but things are looking dicey."

Everyone reported to their regular jobs the following day to help in assessing and repairing any storm damage. Mara learned that several of the small animals had either died or were showing distress caused problems and were being harvested, frozen and stored for future consumption. The lower number of animals to feed would also lessen the strain on the limited grain crops. None of animal meat would go to waste, but the sudden decreased rate of harvest could impact the food supply in the future until animal numbers could be brought back to normal.

The biggest losses were with the important outdoor grain crops, which required food supply projections to be reviewed. The grocery software was immediately updated to implement protein, vegetable and grain product rationing, which affected most of their diet. The covered fields fared somewhat better, although there was significant damage to several protective covers and some power cells would need replacing.

Fortunately, storm protectors encased the bee hive pods in time to save the bee population. The urgency now came from propagating and transplanting flowering plants outdoors. It was going to be some time before they had any orchard blossoms for the bees' diets. They would need to be fed supplemental protein packs as necessary.

During the following days the Helpers and autonomous plows and planters were out in force. The seedlings from the indoor growing rooms were readied for planting. The Manufacturing center was notified with the specifications and numbers to immediately begin to build or repair covers for the fields. Mara and Cali worked wherever Larón needed an extra pair of hands. Krey was working long hours, but seemed reluctant to talk about his assignments. The first grocery drones arrived a few days later with an alarmingly sparse shipment of supplies. Fresh groceries were half the normal order, supplemented with a stack of nutrition bricks, the brown squares Mara recognized from her travel time.

Excessive body mass was unknown on Cytar, so everyone quickly felt the rationing. The human mind was a fickle being, she decided. She had never before thought much about food. It was something she ate when it was time, for her health or the infrequent social experience of dining with others. Now that there was a food problem, she thought more about meals and noticed her hunger. Because she was so busy, any such thoughts of food had to be forced aside so she could stay focused on her job.

No one talked openly about food or eating. Some hoped that ignoring the topic would decrease the thoughts of being constantly hungry, while others feared that openly acknowledging the decreased food rations would only intensify a dangerous situation. Despite all that was happening, the stoic work efforts of everyone strengthened their resolve to survive and eventually thrive.

But the extent of the future rationing was yet to be told.

38

Ridgeway had hoped the storm would lose some intensity as it traveled, but it was not the case. Larón had inspected their food facilities, which grew most of Cytar's oat crop, reporting that they suffered a loss of over half of their yield. They were repairing and replanting at much the same rate as the other complexes, but were at a disadvantage because of the extent of the damage. Krey and Mara were asked to check on the Apogeeway complex and take some requested supplies.

In the early morning, a hauler transport was loaded and picked them up at the Food Production station. Mara eyed the design of this long, streamlined vehicle, with the cargo compartment behind the passenger seats. Krey engaged the high-speed mode, and they sat back and watched as they traversed over monotonous scenery. Once they traveled beyond the Gateway satellites, the ground appeared barren of plant life, although their speed did not allow close inspection.

They passed rocks, crags, stone outcrops and deep, dry channels. The transport traveled low over the ground on its preprogramed route, but even at its high rate of speed, the journey took almost three hours. The dreary landscape lulled her into drowsiness. She welcomed Krey's occasional narrations when something instructive crossed his mind.

"All three of the core sites here are identical, built with the same design program for efficiency and conservation of materials. They each have capacity for more people in hopes that someday our populations will expand."

"And the satellite stations, are they all identical as well?"

"No, not exactly. Each has a specialty, if you will, probably based on the geological features of their location."

As if to illustrate the point, the first sight of a manmade structure came into view, giving respite from the tedious scene, even though the few low buildings looked pitifully small against the vast landscape. The next area resembled large water bubbles sitting low on the horizon. It was the largest satellite development Mara had seen.

"We're passing the largest manufacturing site on Cytar," Krey explained. "They process ores and minerals and have a facility for big equipment. They're in the beginning stages of building our new long-journey transport, the *Pathfinder,* which will be started here and be expanded near the *Superstes'* orbit. Our site is working on the smaller components. I'm not sure how much of their production had to be halted to focus on food production requests due to the storm."

They passed this satellite campus and the main complex and continued until the transport slowed and entered the underground entrance to the Apogee Food Production station. Helpers immediately came to unload the boxes while Krey and Mara entered the building. A wiry, gray-haired man named Jemson introduced himself and thanked them for coming while leading them to a small reception area.

"Please take a few minutes to relax and freshen up while I get some refreshment for us." He returned several minutes later with some drinks and nutrition biscuits. Mara recognized the green drinks she was once offered and had bypassed, but times were different now, and she was hungry. The drinks and biscuits were tastier than anticipated, perhaps the result of her ravaging hunger, and were somehow satisfying her need for food at the moment. She felt more focused as they began their tour. Jemson led them outside to a four-seat ground cart where they drove up a pathway to the grain fields. Workers and Helpers were repairing and testing crop covers.

"Our two main crops at Apogeeway are rice and quinoa. We were extremely lucky in our timing in that we had just harvested one of our rice fields before the storm and had not yet replanted. However, we have lost some of our legume enriched and viable top soil, which had been developed over years and will take time to replenish. Also, one of our other fields suffered major damage when the cover failed. It is being repaired now, and the other field is being prepared for planting."

The low autonomous cultivators were moving through the field as they passed it.

"The new rice plants are being prepared now inside. The AI arms are picking the seedlings, while keeping their roots in a small amount of soil before being transplanted here."

"Where do you get enough water here to grow rice," Mara asked, while Krey wondered what in her memory prompted that question.

Jemson answered, "Our rice doesn't need that much water. We have ample AI vehicles that can keep weeds under control, if we ever get to the point of having a weed problem, so we never flood the fields. We have good success with rice as long as the weather leaves us alone. We just need to expand our fields and grow more of it."

They drove on to another section with the quinoa fields. One intact field was being examined to determine how it survived unscathed, while the next suffered a partially torn cover resulting in a severely mutilated crop.

"The quinoa variety we've developed is very hardy and is an essential part of our diet with its good proteins and minerals. You can see that we've modified the species to produce more of the edible seeds on smaller, less thirsty plants. We continue to try to shorten the time to harvest. We grow the main quinoa crop for all the three colonies, and we're trying to expand our yield. Your group grows the majority of the wheat, and Ridgeway grows their low growing dwarf corn and oats for all of us. I contacted their Food Production, and their storm loss is near catastrophic. I haven't heard exactly what their plan is for reconstruction, but I know they are working as rapidly as possible."

They circled back to the indoor facility which Mara was eager to see. She walked through the area while Krey stayed and talked with Jemson in his office. She learned that neither Apogeeway nor Ridgeway had small animals, making her realize how important Gateway's small animal site was to all the colonies. The hydroponic rooms were similar to theirs, and she found the rice and quinoa seedling areas fascinating. She was hoping that someday all the grain fields could be expanded at Gateway. This site was also very successfully growing rows upon rows of hydroponic tomatoes, laden with the small, red fruit with enough yields to supply not abundant, but adequate amounts to the other towns.

When she met back with Krey, he had finished his review with Jemson and was talking with Lor. He gave Krey an update on the work being done on the *Superstes*, which all seemed to be going as planned. Six crew and six helpers were working on the ship and were expected to be able to complete updates and cleaning within the month. There were no plans currently for another long voyage, and Lor had sounded relieved.

The hauler transport, now loaded with a meager allotment of rice and quinoa, was summoned for the trip back to Gateway. They were each given a container of water and another nutrition biscuit for the journey home. Mara was tired and hungry, but Krey was there, her rock, her model of uncomplaining strength, and he gave her hope when she felt dejected.

They both would need courage to face the upcoming days.

39

The cruelest blow came from a weather abnormality on a day when the light rose with ethereal beauty. With the briefest of warnings, steady breezes began increasing until winds from the east and north began swirling erratically and abruptly joined near Apogeeway, creating full blown and fierce tornadic winds. The system, narrowly focused, yet ferocious, seemed almost on a mission to prove its superiority and bring the colonies into submission by its choice of targets.

It bypassed the main facilities and, just as the residents thought they had escaped harm, the whirling mass of destruction turned, aimed its salvo, and plowed through grain fields. The newly constructed covers of two quinoa plantings were destroyed, the plants left shredded. One entire planting of rice was left in tatters. The psychological effect was as equally damaging as the physical.

Now the suffering would continue longer than anticipated, now the everyday work would become more tedious, the nights would seem drearier. Food began to dominate all thought, with everything now seen through a lens of hunger. Days had turned into weeks and the food rationing continued and tightened. Everyone had lost weight, and although complaining would be futile, the topic of food somehow now seemed to come up more in conversations and eventually even in dreams. The energy put forth at work, even with more forced effort, showed a slow decline, and each person went home exhausted and slept more. The will to survive, however, remained strong. When there was no choice, it was strange how one could force the mind to push aside the gnawing appetite and go on with the most necessary daily activities.

It had become a matter of survival, and the consequence of their isolation in the universe bore into minds. No one could come and rescue them. They could either give up or work harder; they were to survive or perish on their own volition.

As the days wore on, it became harder to hide the distress as the specter of hunger invaded their thoughts. The land began looking bleaker to the tired minds and hungry bodies, while the food rations seemed to shrink and become more tasteless. Hunger colored their days, painted their thoughts and stained their dreams.

Krey, normally untiring, was showing the strain of the meager rations, becoming even more serious and withdrawn. The frustration of his inability to alleviate their hunger was a bitter reminder of how cruel life could be on this alien planet. The normally smiling Mara found it increasingly difficult to maintain her sanguine personality and keep concerns to herself.

On a miserable day that felt as heavy as stone, she looked out and saw sweet Rocket, lying lethargically with ribs protruding. When he looked up at her and gave a tired tail wag, her mood plummeted and her last drops of fortitude seemed to evaporate. She went to visit Gracelyn in hopes of improving her mood, but once they were alone, she broke down and succumbed to despair.

"Are we going to make it through this? We're always hungry and tired. All I want to do is sleep. I keep thinking of what could happen if we get another super storm and lose more food sources."

Gracelyn was watching her, and Mara thought how thin she looked. Her wrists protruding from her shirt looked like skin covered sticks attached to emaciated hands, and yet, her friend always remained outwardly steadfast and strong.

"Oh Mara, we can't give up hope. The people who survive difficult times are the people who never give up hope," she said. "When I need some strength, I think of the earlier settlers who went through much worse suffering than we're going through now, and the few prevailed because they kept a strong mindset. So many people have sacrificed so much, including their lives, for us to be here. We will endure this and get through it. We have no choice. Each day will get better. It gives me hope when I see how hard everyone is working. Never lose hope. We'll take one day at a time and not think of things we can't control now."

Mara was looking at Gracelyn's hand, resting on her arm and, when she lifted her eyes, she saw the mere wisp of the woman, yet she sensed her core of steel conviction. It almost pulsed through her hand into Mara, a strength forged in a hostile environment and honed by unwavering perseverance. Gracelyn smiled a weary smile, but her eyes conveyed such confidence that Mara felt almost ashamed of her anxiety. Her friend's unwavering faith soothed her troubled mind.

Mara smiled back at her friend and squeezed her hand. "One day at a time," she repeated.

But, how many more days, she wondered.

40

A stunning confirmation of genuine hope arrived the next day, when Mara opened her reader to find an announcement from Genna. She was to be bonded with Chad, the man she had spoken about at the appreciation dinner, and Mara and Krey were invited to the private ceremony the following week. Here, in the middle of hunger and distress, this couple remained hopeful, refusing to become disheartened and looking forward to a better future together.

Krey, dressed in dark pants and shirt, accompanied Mara, wearing her red dress, to the ceremony at the Meditation Center. Omi and Lan had already arrived and were visiting with another couple from Genna and Chad's work. The room was an enlarged version of the Meditation room on the *Superstes*, complete with religious symbols and chairs. Mara stared for some time at two beautiful stained-glass windows, before she recognized them as perfect digital representations of glass. The many decorative, deeply colored shapes were surrounding a beautifully depicted angel, a lamb, and white and yellow flowers, complete with the digital shading mimicking three-dimensional art.

The couples sat and visited quietly while soft electronic music played in the background, until the vicar entered with Genna and Chad. Genna was wearing the long gown she wore at the appreciation dinner, and Chad wore a dark shirt and pants, although the clothes on both, as well as the attendees, hung as loosely as oversized clothes on mannequins. The guests stood and formed a semicircle around the couple while they listened to the vicar's words, no one more attentively than Mara. These were the words she barely heard at her own bonding, so distraught she was at the suddenness of it all and the prospect of being with Draven.

It was a longer ceremony than her abbreviated service, with beautiful readings of love, life, commitment and hope. The wrist bracelet segment was identical, and while the bracelets were joined and vows were said, the three witness couples placed their hands over their partner's pledging mark on their wrist. Genna and Chad looked so happy, and Mara hoped Chad was as fine a man as Krey.

Then, to accentuate the significance of the day, the astonished guests were each offered a celebratory drink and a small piece of honey cake to honor the couple. Eyes widened and exclamations went out at the extravagant offerings during a near famine. In between bites of the decadent treat, glasses were raised to honor the couple. "To Genna and Chad, happiness always! Best wishes for the future!"

The laughter and visiting which followed were like a balm to weary friends. The ceremony became an inoculation against the virus of despondency. Now, the small group spoke of the future with a lightness which seemed to shine through the present-day gloom. The times were difficult, but the significant cheerfulness made the bonding all the more special and memorable. The fragility of life and all of its unforeseen events seemed to be held back momentarily, while hope gained ground. It was a welcomed, happy occasion giving respite from a stressful time, with a chance to focus on positive thoughts and the mental fuel needed to endure and persevere.

The bit of hopefulness stayed for several long weeks after the ceremony, nourishing the spirit until the grocery deliveries began slowly, slowly increasing the food allotments. Gradually, the diminished portion packets of soy products, lentils, legumes and prepared food improved and increased while the protein bricks were replaced with more tasty products.

The week that a small container of olive oil and four eggs were included in the delivery felt like a cause to celebrate a momentous occasion. Their bodies were craving fats, and their small emergency rations of oil and sardines had seemed barely enough to sustain life and had become almost a cruel tease. How long had it been since they had tasted fresh eggs? The thought of them kept surfacing in Mara's mind throughout the day with each hunger pang.

For dinner that night she scanned two packets of lentils with tomato, Krey's with the larger caloric portion, into the cooking appliance before turning her attention to the treasured eggs. She stared at them, cradled one lovingly, surprised by her emotions, while deciding they were too precious to be relegated to the all-cook. On the heat surface she sautéed a small packet of chopped onion with the slices of one tiny pepper and set them aside before almost reverently cracking the eggs into a bowl and mixing. A few drops of treasured olive oil were added to the pan before the eggs were poured in for a slow cook and gentle stirring. When the eggs were almost set, she placed the vegetables in a neat row down the middle of eggs before they were carefully rolled over, creating a beautiful omelet. Her mouth was watering when she called Krey from the study. He came into the room to find that she was already sitting at the table staring at her plate. Both were thinking they could easily eat the entire omelet. They gave a prayer of gratitude, which can only be appreciated by those who have gone without, then laughed and gave a tribute toast with a loaded forkful. They had learned to eat very slowly to make the small meals last longer, and especially tonight, to enjoy and relish every delicious bite with a thankful feeling that the worst of the rationing must be over.

That night after dinner, Krey was reading in the sitting room when Mara joined him on the small sofa, kicking off her shoes and curling her feet up under her. She opened her reader to learn more about plant survival in extreme cold. He read for a while, but he found himself watching her out of the corner of his vision, and his mind became thoughtful. He thought of the days before he met her, when he had been driven by work to help secure and improve their precarious existence on this planet. He had been so consumed by maintaining the fragile balance of life in this remote world, he never realized that the intense focus on work had become his armor, covering a veil of aloneness in this infinite space.

He watched her absently twirl a strand of hair behind her ear and thought how the woman who had become his wife was evolving into a loving partner, one that was mentally strong enough to prevail in difficult times. He wasn't even sure what had initially attracted her to him. Oh, she was attractive, but he had been with other attractive women only to find they eventually bored or annoyed him.

He thought back to his first meetings with her on the ship, and how he had immediately felt some innate need to protect her. He was drawn to some depth of character he saw in the attentive ways she responded to all the new experiences she encountered. She was sweet and kind, but he knew there was a core of strength inside her. And now, she was becoming self-assured in her work and home roles, making intelligent and caring decisions without drama. God, how he hated the drama and pettiness in some women. He had to give credit to the programmers and selection teams who evaluated the new Candidates. Once again, they had brought some very steady, good people back with them; people who would help contribute to their life here.

Mara looked up just then, perhaps sensing his gaze.

"What?" she asked, as her easy smile lit up her face.

"Nothing," he said. "Just thinking how pleasant this is, sitting here with you."

She moved closer to him and curled up to continue her reading. *A lucky man.*

41

Minds and bodies responded quickly to the improved diets and increased calories. Gaunt faces filled out, smiles and laughter became more frequent, energy levels increased, moods elevated with the exaltation of survival, while the general atmosphere of the complex transformed from determined perseverance to optimism. Mara and Roz reconnected to visit on their walks or runs now that their energy level improved. Gracelyn and Bertie, as bright and steady as ever, came over for an occasional lunch or dinner, and Rocket's ribs could no longer be felt through his furry coat.

The concern now was the lack of any rain since the storm, but the underground reservoirs were currently maintaining decent levels. The drought tolerant crops which were developed were paying off in their water conservation. Mara was even beginning to think it was near time to resubmit her idea of an experimental green space while she continued to gather information on soils and possible hardy plant choices. The planet's seed banks had been called upon after The Great Storm, as it had been named. The food production stations felt that they still maintained adequate seed inventory. Mara had only to decide when she should bring up the idea again. She began sending concise notes to Larón about some of her readings along with information about a few of the trees and shrubs on which she wished to start her experiments.

She now had the energy to study more about plant DNA and genetically engineering plant cells, and she dedicated much of her evening time to research. All of their edible plants were now engineered to produce more in less than desirable conditions. Much of the information she needed for her idea was familiar to her from her work at Food Production. They had identified genes that carried desirable traits, copied and inserted them into the genome of their food crops. Her goal was to start this process with some of the non-edible plants from the seed bank. Her plan was to use some of the genes from native plants already growing on Cytar and identify which traits allowed them to survive the freezing temperatures.

The tormented little species which had survived the storm were gradually recovering and putting on new growth. The plants near the houses were inspected often, as if willed to grow from Mara's loving attention. She watched the tiny promising leaf buds swell and emerge, and the small pointy blades of grasses poke through the uninterested soil.

A spot of bright butterscotch caught her attention one morning and, on closer inspection, Mara was looking at what she considered a true miracle. On a ground-hugging, rusty, green plant, bloomed the most delicate, exquisite blossom. Five miniature, almond shaped petals sat in perfect symmetry on a serpentine stem. Down on her knees for closer inspection, Mara stared in near disbelief. She turned her head and glanced across the sparse land, a tear sliding down her cheek from the pure joy of seeing such beauty in an otherwise bare vista. Surely this was a sign of more life to come.

When she stood up, a clear, sudden flash of bright flower images crossed her mind. She closed her eyes trying to see the vibrant blooms again, to save them in her strange memory bank, the colorful and large blossoms, so unlike the small tenuous plants here. She wondered what locked vault in mind housed such beautiful sights. She desperately wanted her full memory restored but, for now, she had to believe she was in this new world for a purpose.

She began to observe the plants' foliage just when the light slipped beneath the horizon, causing the temperatures to plummet. With her long coat bundled tightly, she would go out early in the morning and watch the leaves almost reluctantly unfurl when the light mercifully brought the first promise of warmth. The plants' adaptation to its unique climate was remarkable. The soft, delicate looking side of the foliage presented its face to light, but the underside, a layer of thicker, tougher cells curled up tightly and closed in the dark, as if insulating the weak half sibling from the menacing cold. That was the trait she would need in her park plants if they were to survive.

After much discussion with his associates, Larón surprised Mara by informing her via a reply to one of her messages to him. A few seeds from the vault would be made available for her research. Mara's yelp brought Krey out of his office in panic mode. He started to ask what was wrong when he saw the look of jubilation on her face.

"Larón just gave me the go-ahead for my green park idea. He's letting me experiment with three species of plants! If anything shows promise, they will eventually build a small protective space to begin the experiments."

"That's terrific. It means they have a great deal of confidence in your abilities."

"I know, it's a big responsibility. It's all going to be so experimental, trying to get Earth plants to survive in this climate, with only limited protection from the severe temperature changes."

"You've had a vision for this, so now's your chance. Larón and his team like the idea or they wouldn't have approved it. You should feel honored if that group gives sanction to your idea. Just don't get discouraged; it'll take time. You'll have to read some of the old journals if you ever feel like things are hopeless. I have faith in you, just remember it will take time, years, but like in all endeavors, you have to start somewhere and persevere."

42

Krey, now back to his full work routines both on and off site, was working in his home office one afternoon when Lor's face came up on a screen. "Are you available for a call?"

Krey's hand passed over the respond bar, and the screen divided, with his face now visible to Lor.

"I'm here, how's it going in Apogee? Getting anything to eat over there?"

"That's barely amusing after what we've all been through, but yes, we're all pretty much at normal caloric rations. I'm wondering if you're up for a little inspection jaunt with Tanak and me. We need to get up to the *Superstes* and do the final check before the work crews come home and the deep space monitoring crew takes their first stationary rotation."

"Wow, that's springing one on me. Normally I'd jump at the chance, and I still want to go, but I need to make sure Mara feels secure with it. How long do you expect to be away?"

"Well, figure a day each way travel, and hopefully we can get everything done in three days, maybe four, so we'll shoot for five, maybe six days total, barring any problems. We'll be taking the next station crew with us. They'll stay on board when we bring the work team home."

"Sounds good. When were you thinking of leaving?" He was already thinking about how to tell Mara.

"Day after tomorrow, if that works for you. I'm monitoring the weather conditions. We could possibly push it back one more day, but the work crew is anxious to get back, I'm sure."

"Okay, should be fine, but let me get back to you. I want to let Mara know what's going on."

"Let me know as soon as you can so I can alert the Ctransport team. They're on standby now and proceeding with all the preflight work as we speak. Talk to you soon."

Lor's side of the screen went dark.

Krey waited until after dinner, while considering how to tell Mara of his plans. They were putting their few dishes in the cleaning cabinet when he decided the direct way would be best.

"Lor called today and said the work crew on the *Superstes* is finished with all the updating, and they need him, Tanak and me to go and inspect the ship before they leave."

She turned quickly and looked at him with a wary expression.

"When would that be? For how long?" The questions he knew would come.

"I think it needs to be soon, maybe in a couple days, so the work crews can come home. Won't be for long; maybe only five days or so." Her eyes widened in surprise.

"Wow, that's soon." She was thinking of the night sky and how far away he would be. Then she had another thought, and her face brightened.

"Could I go with you?"

Now it was his turn to be surprised as he searched for an answer. He had been proud of her adjustment and transformation in this new life and now saw her in the new light, no longer the newly awakened, weak, confused person, but a clearer thinking, stronger, more confident woman. He struggled with the wording, but finally just said it.

"I can't take you with me. You wouldn't want to come anyway—you know what it's like there. Nothing new, just work for the three of us. Besides, you have your own work here."

She was frowning, pondering the pros and cons of the journey. She knew that she had lived in only a small part of the ship, and had never even seen its exterior. She did not relish the idea of going on the trip, but she did not like the thought of him being so far away. Krey could see she was relenting.

"I can talk to you whenever all the communication paths stay open. Gracelyn and Bertie will be here. And Rocket." He walked over and put his arms around her. "You'll be fine; I won't be gone that long."

She had a resolute look on her face when she finally said, "I'll be fine. I hope the trip doesn't drag out."

"Hopefully, it should all be routine, and I'll be home when expected."

"Can I at least go with you to the flight complex and watch you take off? Are you traveling on the Ctransport?"

"No, actually we're taking one we affectionately call our ferry transport because it's smaller and used primarily for shuttling workers and a few supplies back and forth. The Cytar transport is for larger cargo hauls and can accommodate more people. You can come to the flight station, but you can't enter the flight center where we prepare for take-off. Might not be worth your time."

"Let me think about it," she said, but she had already made up her mind.

When the departure morning arrived, Mara rode to the flight station with Krey. They stood outside the building, embraced in a strong hug, not talking, until he kissed her goodbye and walked inside. She watched him enter the building, strong shouldered, with his travel bag slung across his back, always looking ahead.

Instead of going straight to work, she directed the Gsport to the viewing lot, marked only by two signs in the level dirt. She surmised that the lot would be full of family members and interested citizens if there were a major expedition underway, but now the Gsport was the solo vehicle parked, facing the building.

She reviewed data on her reader while she waited for over an hour before a sleek looking craft slowly emerged into view and traveled a good distance from the building, stopping near where the ground rose into a gently sloping hill. This transport was smaller than the one she arrived on, but still impressive in size. Its black color shone with an iridescent purple, giving it an almost dangerous appearance.

She knew that Krey, Lor, Tanak, and the rotation crew would be strapped in their seats, and she said a silent prayer for their safety. She expected more noise before the takeoff, but her only clue to the initial sequence was seeing brief and almost invisible heat waves appearing in the air behind the shuttle transport. And then, the rapidity of the takeoff was breathtaking. As if being released from a tether, it shot forward, swiftly gaining speed, briefly following the land topography to the upward slope, then immediately shooting outward at incredible speed. In less than a minute, she was gazing at a dot in space, straining her eyes until the dot disappeared, and feeling alone as she rode to work.

43

Lor, as lead pilot, communicated with the flight station during the first hour, confirming the computer's accurate trajectory to the *Superstes*. Everyone now could remove their helmets, worn for a safety precaution during takeoff and landing. The six-member station crew was seated behind the cockpit cabin and settled in for the duration. They had a long idle time stretching before them with no gravity and a relatively small area to move, float, and stretch in their sections of the transport. Sometimes they talked, rested or slept, taking turns getting out of their seats.

When all the systems' operations satisfied Lor, he switched his communication feed to include the open cabin.

"I received some interesting information from our ground procurement team. According to them, our Cytar communities have surpassed the Mars station in terms of advancement and livability."

"That's surprising and disturbing," Tanak replied. "Especially considering how much longer they've been established. I'm wondering if they've stopped funding them altogether. I hope they don't end up being abandoned! Their news sources would never inform people if they did."

"Those poor people. They'll have an even more miserable life without the proper support." Krey said grimly. "Our advancement is directly linked to our huge advantage of the breathable atmosphere; not the same as Earth, but close enough, and our bodies have adapted. They don't even have the basics for sustainability without backing from Oneworld."

"I know you've got that right, but they have an almost eight decades head start on us," Tanak went on. "They should have some nice facilities by now. It was really strange going back this last time. I've always thought of Cytar's development as being fairly basic, but, the one time I was back to Mars Base briefly on the last mission, it was alarming to see the dark, primitive base there. So strange, they have great technology and yet their outpost is just depressing. Drab buildings, terrible lighting, massive blinding spotlights in between pitch-black gaps. I couldn't wait to get back to the *Superstes*."

"The problems seem to stem from Oneworld not wanting to fund any improvements," Lor added. "According to our team, they only want to increase appropriations for mining the precious metals. They're using more AI units and fewer humans. The AI units have all but taken over, and they don't need anything in the way of creature comforts. More robotic use is understandable considering the harsh conditions, but they still should be doing more for the humans than they are. They're drafting workers for both the moon and Mars stations now, because they are getting no volunteers to support their Helpers. Our guys said the conditions are pretty tough there. I think that's why our team was so readily able to get the fed-up workers to help them travel covertly and obtain supplies."

Krey was looking at a monitor of black space and stars which extended into infinity. He could understand the need and the wisdom behind the difficult decisions made by the early space pioneers. It had to be painfully challenging to leave their home in a desperate hope of finding some unknown inhabitable planet. His thoughts turned to Tanak and the Creos.

"Tanak, weren't you on the Creotarn survival ship years ago that met our *Navigator*?"

"I was barely two years old and remember nothing of it. Probably a blessing. I just remember a few stories that my parents told me of the chaos on Creotarn, and how they escaped on a crowded transport. So much difficulty and sacrifice on that trip. They were on near starvation rations, not knowing if they would ever find a habitable planet. It had to be by the grace of God that we met the *Navigator*.

Tanak looked out his small window for a few moments before continuing.

"My mother told me that the *Navigator* took almost 200 of us on board to help alleviate our overcrowded conditions and extend the food, but that meant sacrifice for them, sharing limited food, terrible crowding. We followed your ship to Cytar, and just in time, as both ships had limited supplies, air filtration was strained; our ship was in poor shape, and the power cells were beginning to deteriorate from the long journey. The good news is we were able to salvage so much technology from it and used its parts to incorporate into your shuttle and Ctransports. We still have the remaining scrap from it and occasionally still find it useful."

Krey was picturing the events in his head. He could not imagine how horrible the conditions must have been on the overcrowded vessels.

"And to think we've never heard another signal or encountered another ship since."

Lor interrupted at this point.

"Don't you remember the excitement about a dozen or so years ago, when we detected a fast radio burst? Two actually, but the second was even fainter than the first. They were extremely brief pulses which were determined to be millions of light years away, but it really got the physicists buzzing for a while. And since then, nothing."

"That's probably a good thing if my home was any example," Tanak said. "Creotarn was self-destructing, with powerful people vying for yet more power, developing all manner of weapons, the cruelest being the bio-weapons delivering painful, lingering deaths. Such a shame, so much loss."

Krey said, "Your scientists have been a Godsend. They've helped us in so many areas. They compressed our time line for advanced energy and medicine. Our life would be more challenging without your people, and we're grateful."

"Well, we wouldn't have survived without you, so it's mutual." Tanak got up and moved to the back of the small cabin, signaling the end of the conversation.

Krey eventually fell asleep and slept until he heard Lor speaking to the crew on the *Superstes*. He consulted his monitors only to find they still had almost four hours until they could land. This was the part of trip where he always became antsy and needed to stretch often. He was not used to sitting for so long and not being actively engaged in work. He knew this tour and every space flight was a near miracle, but at this stage of every trip, his body wanted to move and his mind often yielded to ennui. In his feeble attempt to combat it, he moved around, ate a prepared meal, talked to crew members, read for a while, and played some mindless games, until his monitoring screen, and then his little window, began to reveal the magnificence of the spacecraft coming into view.

44

The ship coming into sight was a beautiful beast. She was a glorious piece of architecture, built for an unforgiving atmosphere, yet still functional and somehow majestic in its size and strength. It never ceased to fill Krey with awe. All three men sat in silence taking in the mammoth sight emerging before them. They knew she didn't always look like this. First came the smaller builds from Cytar, linked in space and used almost as space workshops, until they slowly completed sections which were fused permanently together. This distance traveler did not have the wieldy arms of the old stationary orbiters.

This beauty's profile somewhat resembled an overgrown, stronger, more menacing version of their shuttle's. This creature's massive one-story rugged nose gradually grew in height as it swept back and rose until it met the three-story middle habitation section, a huge circular assembly rising just above the fore and aft sections. The low profile 360° bridge seemed small in proportion to the body. The stern of the ship angled nicely from the broad, middle body section, continuing back until maintenance tunnels, exhaust bays, and defense ports came into view. The elongated length was somehow perfectly proportioned to its impressive width and height. The ample docking bays, barely visible, appeared as slim projections from both sides of the aft unit, spreading out like small extensions hugging a fuselage. Their angular shapes were dwarfed by the main body. Only the circular midsection enjoyed gravity, leaving over half of the ship gravity free, including the areas containing the power cores, life support equipment and huge cargo bays.

Superstes, Survivor.

It was an appropriate name. Here was a world unto itself in an endless space, where every square foot must have purpose to support the physical and mental needs of its crew. She was their last remaining ship, the survivor, capable of deep space travel, and they had only the three smaller transports, which must double as defense crafts if the need ever arose. One of those stayed on the mother ship at all times in case of emergencies.

Losing the *Navigator* and its auxiliary crafts was a tremendous loss, leaving them dangerously underequipped in a hostile environment. It would take decades to build another ship with deep-space travel capabilities. They were expanding the manufacturing site and already in the beginning stages of a new deep space craft, but resources on Cytar always had to be focused first on the immediate needs of life support, food and shelter.

All three men were monitoring screens as they approached the ship, while Lor communicated with a docking Helper. They watched port side docking bay doors slowly retract as they synced orbits with the destination craft. The approach looked deceivingly slow, even though they were traveling around Cytar at thousands of miles per hour. As they entered the docking bay, lights on the display illuminated, warning that autopilot had been disengaged. Lor lowered the undercarriage docking coils and carefully watched his screen, matching the coils with the landing circles on deck before resting the ship completely down on the flight deck. Huge clamps emerged from the flight deck of the mother ship and locked on the rings securing their smaller spacecraft.

The cockpit had been silent while Lor concentrated on the landing, but Krey started with a good-natured banter as soon as it touched down.

"What's the matter, Lor, you don't trust our AI systems? Why didn't you just sit back and have the autopilot land the shuttle, huh, not good enough for you?"

"What's the fun in that? Besides, I need to keep my skills up with the manual flight. You never know when I might need them in an emergency, and then you'd be praising my skills from now to forever and be thankful that I practiced when I could." He was grinning while he checked the system lights. "Plus, flying these overgrown space animals is fun."

He was used to the kidding about his love of space piloting. Besides, they knew his computer interfacing was always connected to the flight sensors and could be engaged in a nanosecond if his thoughts required it. The men finished their post flight check as the large bay doors closed behind them. When they heard the Helper announce "Welcome aboard," Lor released the rear door hatch as crew and Helpers began guiding the cables and extending the cylindrical walkway for their transfer to the conversion hall.

Cargo holds were opened and Helpers were already beginning to unload the shipment of supplies which had been carried on the transport. They were placed on enclosed conveyor belts which moved them directly to storage rooms, where they were scanned and sorted to their proper destinations. No matter the mission, all flights to the ship brought supplies to keep the vessel fully stocked.

The passengers made their way to the air lock hall, waiting to sync with the oxygenated entry before removing the durable outer suits and entering the main ship. Helpers were waiting to assist and take their flight suits. Krey was surprised by his initial reaction to being back on board. He usually felt excitement, but his circumstances had changed, and this felt too soon to be back after the long journey. He had just arrived and was already eager to finish this short stay and get back home.

A boisterous greeting of handshakes and back slaps greeted them before they dropped off the travel bags in their cabins. Eventually, they made their way to a dining area to eat and get caught up on news from home. The main topic of conversation was The Great Storm, the crop devastations, the repairs, and subsequent food shortages. For once, the work crew was happy to have been off planet.

After the meal, the visiting, and a brief overview of the next day's work, Krey made his way to one of the small exercise rooms. He needed to move and exert himself after his sedentary day. Afterwards he headed back to his old quarters for a shower and rest. The ship seemed eerily quiet without the full crew and Helpers. He passed the hall leading to new Candidate quarters, and he thought of the first time he saw the newly awakened Mara barely standing in the hall, never imaging at the time, that his life was about to change for the better.

The orbit had taken them to the back side of Cytar, so communication would be closed, unless an emergency required the use of the added power needed for relayed communiques. Their successful docking would have been reported to the crew's registered list of family members or associates. Krey turned in for the night, looking forward to talking with Mara the following morning.

45

Mara, aware that she would not receive any communication from the flight on the first day, was grateful for her work to keep her busy and focused. Gracelyn and Bertie had kindly asked her to join them for dinner on her first night alone. The two connected home's floorplans mirrored each other, making it easy for Mara to feel familiar with the surroundings. Even the furniture was a clone of their house, with only slightly different color tones. This was no doubt a necessity in an environment with limited resources, where customization was an unknown luxury.

The evening with Gracelyn and Bertie generated the warmth and hominess that only comes from being with good friends, but it was still strange to return to her empty house with the knowledge of how distant she was from Krey. The pleasant visit helped her to sleep well, and she received his call just before she left for work the next morning. She learned that the flight had gone well and the team was ready to begin the inspections.

After hearing Mara's normal and upbeat sounding voice, Krey felt reassured and ready to for the day when he met everyone for breakfast. The inspections were divided for the day. Several of the reviews involved working in the gravity free and lower oxygen zones of the ship. This presented little concern for the men aside from a few precautions, namely adjusting the magnetic level of the no-gravity boots or using supplemental oxygen when needed, and always being aware that supplies were locked into specific places.

The on-board work team had been in constant communication with the flight center on Cytar, so their jobs were continually reviewed remotely. Lor's team was sent with specific areas for more in-depth on-site evaluation. When they reviewed the almost overwhelming list of duties, they began to wonder if it could be accomplished in just a few days. They, too, would need to be in direct communication with the scientists on standby at the flight center and would be relying heavily on Helpers.

Krey was meeting with two of the work team at the computer core in the protected deep interior of the ship. He needed to inspect the new hardware and updates, and he was facing a long, tedious day. Tanak was starting in the medical and Candidate bays before moving on to general crew quarters. They each set off to their prospective stations, each with a Helper to record their information and reports.

Lor's first task was to inspect the new power cells and their updates. While they stayed in orbit around Cytar, they would be using the hydrogen oxygen fuel cells which could convert the released water vapor into a portion of their drinking water. During the long journey missions, in addition to electromagnetic propulsion, they could switch to inertial fusion which could release colossal energy when needed. He was to check and verify the data from the latest generation of these energy sources and had three Helpers assisting with the figures.

The radiation shields had been reinforced and needed to be reviewed with the work team. Exposure to the amounts of radiation during deep space travel was a continuing concern. Every crew member was monitored during and after a mission with particular attention given to any deterioration in their chromosomal telomeres. The shields seemed to offer adequate protection, but they were constantly upgraded as new research dictated. The updates to the highly sophisticated oxygen generating and water reclamation systems would also be reviewed along with the backup systems. All systems required redundancy in space.

As he was walking the halls to the computer cores, Krey glanced at one of the signs pointing to the escape pods. He knew they were also located in two other areas along the perimeter of the ship, but he wondered if they were only on board for emotional support. They were the equivalent of lifeboats on ocean transports, with one glaring difference. People on lifeboats had air to breathe and other humans on a finite planet. He wondered how long anyone in an escape pod would last without another transport to pick them up, and the chances of that could be very remote. He hoped they would never need to be used.

The work continued nonstop with only the briefest break for a quick lunch. At the end of the day, the mentally exhausted men all met for dinner. So far, everything was checking out with no problems to report. They turned in early, ready for some rest before starting again in the morning. Krey was able to get a brief call in to Mara, and he told her he would check in again the following evening.

In the early morning hours, she woke up two hours early after a bizarre dream and was unable to fall back asleep. She listened to the common night winds sweeping over the house, while something in the fading dream was plaguing her memory, denying her rest. She stayed in bed with her eyes open looking at the blank darkness, and her mind began to wander down avenues of work and space.

She thought of her strange journey and wondered where she came from and why she could not remember. She knew that it is seldom wise to ruminate in the middle of the night, when the dark-loving worries can sprout and grow unhindered by the light. Her mind refused to listen to her pleas for stillness. She pondered the fragility of the small communities and how far away everything seemed, and in the darkness, her active mind reveled in creating doubts and concerns.

She welcomed the first light and fairly jumped out of bed to put the negative thoughts away and start the day. She was surprised at how different and better everything seemed in the bright daylight. She must remember that, she told herself, somewhat unconvincingly. For now, the worries had retreated into the back crevices of her mind unable to compete with the busy tasks of the day as she set off to work.

Things were going well at work, and it was a joy to have Cali's instantaneous information at her disposal. The food production was at last back to its pre-storm levels and gradually expanding. She was humbled and excited by the level of respect Larón had shown by entrusting her with the current project of creating synthetic meat on Cytar.

He was very pleased with the progress of her work, which was looking promising. New, viable cattle stem cells had survived on this latest deep space mission, and her lab was developing new palatable proteins which would greatly add to their food supply. The meat products would be a good source of brain nutrients and calories, and having an extra food source would benefit all. The need for additional food supplies had been burned into the entire population's nerves, with the faint flame of starvation fear always flickering within.

46

Mara left work in a surprisingly good mood considering her abbreviated night's sleep. The afternoon was calm, beautiful and clear, enticing her to take Rocket out for a run. She stopped by Roz' house, but finding no one home, she headed out by herself with Rocket running happily ahead. As her trail looped around to return home, she slowed to a walk, never tired of studying the strange landscape. So barren, so silent, she thought, not a single bird, no small mammals, no rivers or tall trees. Harsh. A mistake here is life threatening. And yet, the low light and long shadows created a surprisingly pleasant and comforting scene as she approached the small cluster of homes. Surviving and thriving here brought a deserved feel of accomplishment. The unfertile views always brought her park project back to the foreground of her thoughts. It would be a perfect night to research the microbial needs of the soil in her planting area. The actual genetic work would be done in her lab, but much of the research and lists of needs could be started at home.

She walked through the neighborhood houses in time to see a slow moving Gsport cruising by her house. The windows were too dark to see the occupants, and she soon dismissed the unusual sighting. That night Krey was able to get a quick call in before losing communication. It sounded as if all was going well, and he was still on track to return on schedule. Just as the call ended, she was startled by a loud, deep sound. So rare was the sound, it took a fraction of a second to process the noise as Rocket barking from his kennel. She thought back to the Gsport which had passed by the house earlier, and immediately grabbed her coat, requested the exterior lights and went outside.

"Rocket, what's the matter?" Rocket was looking in the direction of the distant town with hackles up. She was relieved when Bertie came out to check on the noise.

"What's going on? Rocket almost never barks."

They walked in the direction the dog was looking, but saw only a wall of darkness.

"I can't see anything, but he definitely thinks he saw or heard something," Mara said.

"Probably nothing, but it is very uncommon. Are you okay tonight, or do you want to come over for a while?"

"Thanks, but I think I'll be fine. I may bring Rocket in with me tonight. I'll turn on his chip to respond to the dog door, and we should be fine."

"I don't think it's anything, but you know we're right here if you need anything."

"Thanks, Bertie," she said as she released the dog from his kennel and hurried in from the freezing air and plummeting temperatures.

She activated Rocket's implanted chip which would open the dog door when he stood directly in front of it. She went around the house to make sure all of the shades had closed, checked the house systems and felt more secure when

Rocket finally settled down. She laughed at herself for having him inside as she made a blanket bed for him on the floor in the bedroom.

"Don't get any big ideas about staying in here every night. This is strictly a one-time night watchdog job for you."

The dog wagged his tail, turned around on the blanket several times, completely messing it up before lying down. She smiled watching him, thinking of how she had immediately felt a strong connection with this furry personality. She read until she was sleepy and didn't wake up until she heard Rocket shake and yawn in the morning.

By the time she came into the eating area, he was already exploring in the backyard, and everything seemed normal. She returned him to the kennel before she left for work and was looking forward to the day. Her new work on the cow stem cells was going well, and she had plans to meet Genna and Omi for lunch. She had not seen them since Genna's bonding ceremony and was anxious to get caught up on their news.

The morning flew by, and the lunch with friends at a café in the Complex was very pleasant. The women quickly began exchanging work and home news. Omi was working at the medical complex, and Genna seemed happy and was now working at the technology center. She and Chad had their own little apartment near Omi and Lan.

At one point, the conversation briefly turned to the time before their journey here. Mara kept a fixed smile on her face as she listened to the women, as they recalled several of their activities before living here. Genna began to reminisce about all the stress of their former assignments.

"Oh lordie, Mara, remember that night when we had to meet near that creepy abandoned building? I was getting so freaked out, thinking I'd missed you."

Mara's face only reflected an unemotional blankness, causing Genna to change the subject. They quickly launched into memories of life on the transport and laughed over some of their experiences traveling to Cytar, working with the Helpers, and Omi's near perfect emulation of Mopmop's voice. The three women played off of each other's sense of humor with very clever and witty results. The lunch visit passed quickly until all three needed to return to work. They said goodbyes with promises to meet again soon.

Mara walked toward the entrance to meet her Gsport, all the while consciously suppressing bewildering thoughts of her lost memories, which her friends seem to have retrieved. She fought the concerns by purposely observing the condensed, yet pleasant surroundings and the few other people sitting or walking to their destinations. None of this was necessary for survival, she realized. Items here could be ordered from home, but she understood why this was a popular place. The interior of this complex with its green plants and miniature streams and fountains was a welcome contrast to the stark, monochromatic outdoor landscapes.

With her thoughts wandering, she did not immediately become aware of someone following very near to her. When some nebulous warning surfaced, she turned suddenly, surprised to see Draven walking next to her.

"Hello Draven, what are you doing here?"

"Hello, Mara. I just finished lunch and saw you and thought I'd say hello." He was smiling, but he was walking uncomfortably close to her.

She stopped and looked straight at him and said in a very composed voice, "How have you been?"

Draven paused and quickly reassessed his thoughts. This was not the timid, unsure Mara on the ship. This Mara was confident and looked strong and very sure of herself. Often feeling inferior in his adeptness with women, he had become quite successful in the past in choosing women he deemed easy to intimidate. What happened here? This wasn't going as planned. He needed to change his strategy quickly, or he could get into some serious trouble. It would not be smart to cause any issues which would upset Krey.

"I've been great, and you look wonderful," he said in a tone as smooth as soft butter. "How are you and Krey doing? I hear he's out on ship now."

Now more wary, Mara wondered, how does he know that?

"We're fine, things are going well. Yes, Krey's out, supposed to be home tonight or tomorrow, I think." She smiled and kept looking at him, hoping he did not know Krey's schedule. She started walking toward the exit, "Where are you working now?"

"I'm in maintenance, and we're always busy."

"That's a very important job. I'm glad they have good people working there." She was hoping he would understand the compliment.

They had reached the Complex doors and Mara was relieved to see her Gsport waiting. She turned to Draven and gave him a sincere smile. "It was so nice to see you. Take care of yourself, Draven," and she quickly turned around and got into her vehicle.

That was a strange encounter, and she wondered if it had been a coincidental or a planned meeting. But how would he have known she would be there? By the time she arrived at Food Production, her mind was already on her job.

47

Krey was ready to come home. Only one more work day and, hopefully, they could finish the inspections and head home. It was funny how he could tolerate a long mission when he knew the timeline in advance, and he could mentally prepare for that. This short trip was one he wasn't expecting and, in ordinary circumstances, wouldn't have minded. This trip was different. On this trip he kept thinking of Mara at home, and he found himself missing her. He missed talking to her about their day, he missed her smile, and he missed her soft hands on his body. Thankfully, he would be home and see her in less than two days if all went well.

He was able to connect a video call to her and briefly told her about their work. He was mildly disturbed when she mentioned seeing Draven at the Complex, but dismissed his concerns when he saw her normally happy demeanor. He told her he missed her before the video became snowy, and he ended the call with a quick goodbye before staring at a dark screen.

He started the next day with the anticipation of finishing up the work and preparing for the return journey the following morning. The men went to their work assignments, now each with two crew members and the Helpers who would be staying on board for the upcoming space monitoring rotation. The new crew needed to become familiar with the equipment updates, ask questions, and make sure the onboard Helpers were programmed to meet their needs.   When the ferry transport took off in the morning, the six remaining would be responsible for maintenance, plus their work assignments, for the next six to eight months.

Mara's work was going well, and she was looking forward to Krey's return.   She was pleased with the slow, steady progress of the work, even though it meant tedious hours looking at magnified cells, taking meticulous care growing muscle fibers in cultures before experimenting with the additives to produce texture and flavor.   Cali was a big help with data recording and projecting time lines.   With Krey away, Mara was also working longer and adding some research about her plants for her green park idea.

When her brain reached overload, she made a spur of the moment decision to return to the main complex to see if she could get an idea for something to buy for Krey as a little welcome home gift.   She was walking out of the first store with no inspiration, when she heard Draven's voice.

"Well, hello again, two days in a row."

She turned to him as a flash of annoyance raced through her mind.   *Is he following me?*

"This is a coincidence, I'm not really following you," he said, as if reading her thoughts.   He had something in his hands which he kept bending and folding, and he seemed nervous, shifting his weight from one foot to the other.

"Hello," she said in a very neutral tone. Krey would be home soon, and the last thing she wanted to do was spend any time with Draven. She was staring at him with an unsmiling face, thinking she would keep this encounter short.

"I've just needed to talk to you and never could get up the nerve. I don't exactly know how to say this," he went on hesitantly. "I'm embarrassed by my behavior toward you on the ship, and I guess this is my pathetic way to apologize. I chose you for bonding because I was attracted to you, and I thought we could make it work."

He sounded sincere, she thought, somewhat warily. Unwilling to enter into any lengthy discussion, she decided on a quick response.

"Things are working out the way they should, so I guess it's all okay. It seems like we're both doing well and working hard, and that's all good," she replied.

He looked visibly relieved, and his voice sounded more confident. "Thanks. I don't mean to bother you, I really don't. When we were on the ship, things just never seemed to come out the way I meant them. I just started seeing someone from work, and so far, it's going well, and I'm hoping things will work out for us. We had a long talk last night, and she's made me realize I need to apologize to you, that's all."

He shrugged, not knowing what else to say, and took the old folded baseball cap he had been twisting, snapped it

255

open, and put it on. It was a faded denim color with a pale flag symbol in the front, showing worn red, dirty white and blue colors. The cloth on the bill was frayed through in spots and was starting to curl back on the edges.

Mara stared, transfixed. "Where did you get that hat?" She remained spellbound, eyes on the cap, while trying unsuccessfully to remember where she'd seen a similar one.

Draven gave a short laugh. "This old thing? I've had it so long, brought it from back home. It's one of those things that fit great, you know, like an old pair of jeans, and it's got sentimental value, I guess, because I can't seem to let it go."

Something flashed in her brain. She saw a vision of a man in a baseball cap, smiling at her through the slight stubble of a beard. Then, she saw flashes of deep green. Green grass, green trees, green hills.

"Mara, what's wrong? Are you okay? You look so pale, like you're going to faint. Are you feeling sick?" Mara blinked and saw Draven and the hat, and she felt unsteady.

"I just need to get back to my Gsport," she said as she started walking.

"It's this way," he said, afraid to touch her, but pointing behind her.

She turned, leaving him standing, and walked off to the main entrance and into the waiting vehicle. She covered her face with her hands and closed her eyes.

"Would you like to return to work now?" The Gsport's voice asked when it did not receive a command within the programmed time.

Her hands were trembling. Some process in her memory was causing an unsettling disorientation.

"Home" was all she said.

She did not realize she was home until it was announced, and the vehicle door opened. She wandered into the sitting room and sat for a long time, trying to recall more memories. When the room wall sconces illuminated, she realized how late it was and went to the kitchen to heat a cup of soup. She was sitting, staring and thinking, when the call came from Krey.

"Hi, we're leaving tonight in a few hours. Thanks to all the Helper assistance, we finished early, so we're not waiting until tomorrow to leave. I should be home in the early afternoon tomorrow." He sounded happy and full of energy, but became concerned when he heard her subdued tone.

"What's going on, are you okay?"

"I don't know, I think so. Yes, I'm fine, really. I just had some strange memory flashes." Her voice sounded flat. "They scared me, because I couldn't control them. But I think they're gone now, and I'm just glad you'll be home a little early."

Mara felt somewhat comforted from the call, but Krey's head was spinning. This was the real downside of these long distant trips. There was no way to get home any sooner and no way to know exactly what was going on there. He immediately talked to Lor and Tanak, who confirmed that there had been no reported problems from the other

Candidates. Probably just an anomaly which would not be repeated, they assured him. Even their assurances did little to relieve the anxiety, and Krey couldn't get packed and preflight checked fast enough.

The shuttle goodbyes were always a little strange. The homeward bound crew was excited to leave and although the new crew was looking forward to their jobs on board, there was still the initial feeling of isolation on the mother ship once the transport disengaged and headed off.

After the flight pre-check was completed the docking bay doors retracted. As the deck holding clamps were withdrawn Lor initiated a one-second engagement of the forward thrusters, causing the transport to begin a reverse motion. The small backward movement in zero gravity was enough to expedite the unlocked shuttle's direct motion away from the *Superstes* as it continued on its orbit. Once clear of the mother ship, and all systems go, Lor gave a signal to the onboard systems to engage the homeward trajectory. They all settled in for the long flight, which couldn't be finished soon enough for Krey.

48

Mara awoke after a night of contorted dreams and went to work. Keeping her schedule seemed like the best way to keep her mind occupied. She thankfully had no more memory recall issues and was looking forward to Krey's return. All went well until late morning when she looked up from her magnifying screen and felt momentarily dizzy. She shook her head in an effort to relieve the dizziness, when bursts of vivid uncontrollable memories immediately flooded her mind. There was the lake and a boat and brick houses, all flashing before her. She saw snow, and then she was inside a house with wooden beams in the ceiling and a huge rock fireplace, and the vivid images would not stop. She felt nauseous and ill. She took some deep breaths trying to compose herself and finally managed to summon her ride before telling Risha she needed to go out for a while.

The ride home gave no respite from the rushing roulette wheel spinning off images in her brain. She tried looking off in the distance, then covering her eyes, but still they came. She could see herself running and not being able to get away from someone, but she could never identify the person. She saw the man in the ball cap looking down to hand her something, but what was it?

She stumbled into the house and collapsed on the sofa in the sitting room. She closed her eyes, but the room seemed too hot, then too cold and when she tried to open her eyes, the sofa felt as if it were spinning. She closed them tightly and laid there shivering until she fell asleep and entered a vivid dreamland. She was younger in these dreams, happy, laughing, totally engaged in her studies, knowing the answers. Then the images shifted with disturbing rapidity; she was grown and working and swimming and everything became a blurry confusion until she woke herself up.

She sat for a minute trying to sort the images before she came into the present and realized how late it was. Krey should be arriving soon. She needed to see him and needed him to hold her, to tell her she would be all right, and to make the memory flashes stop. She would go to the flight center and meet him.

She stood up and turned toward the door when more sharp memories started flooding into her brain in rapid succession. She saw her home. She saw her vehicle. She saw streets she knew. Her hands went to the sides of her head as if trying to stop the torrents of fractured memories, but they persisted. She saw the man with the ball cap, and suddenly, she knew she cared for him. And then, she ran.

She ran out the door, straight across the drive path, screaming, "Nooo! Stop!"

She clawed her way straight up the protective bank, scrapping her hands, and ran blindly out into the open land. Gracelyn heard the scream and hurried out just in time to see Mara top the bank and bolt away.

"Mara! Mara! Wait! What happened?" she called, but she could see Mara was in no state to stop or listen. She ran back into the house and called Bertie at work. It was then that she saw the notification of the shuttle landing and sent the Gsport off for Krey.

The flight took longer than expected, and now the post flight check seemed to be taking forever before every item was cross-checked. At last, the final confirmation was given and the door released and slowly opened. Lor thanked everyone for their work before the men headed to the final on-site review and release. Krey saw his Gsport and fairly jogged to it, expecting to see Mara.

He was met by an empty vehicle and immediately called her. No answer. Now his concern increased; this didn't seem like her. Something must have happened. He called Gracelyn on the way home, and she explained the little she knew. He tried Mara's wrist comm again to no avail. It was not like her to ignore a call, and according to Gracelyn, she was upset and not on her regular running route. He reached home shortly after Bertie. If exhaustion and fear and worry were to be expressed visually, it would be on Krey's face when the Gsport arrived.

"Do you have any news?"

"No, not yet," Bertie said. "We're tracking her wrist comm, but she's just running out in the middle of nowhere."

Krey raced in the house where he kicked off his shoes and all but tore off his uniform. He threw on pants, a warm shirt and his running shoes before checking Mara's location on his wrist comm.

"I'm going to try and find her before it gets dark," he told Bertie.

Seeing the futility of trying to talk him out of it, Bertie just said, "You don't have that much time. Be careful and watch for the cold." Krey never heard the words, as he ran out the door following Mara's shown location.

Mara was running, stumbling, crying, remembering her home. Why was she here? Who did this? Why didn't anyone tell her? She ran, gasping for breath, at one point stopping and leaning over with her hands on her knees, sobbing. Tanak should have explained more to her. Krey should have told her more, instead of giving such superficial answers to all her questions. She looked up and another painfully abrupt image of crushing crowds shot through her brain. She ran.

Then the anger rose in her. It was an anger that stole her rational judgement. *I don't know where I'm going. I don't care. This is not my home; I don't belong here!* She ripped off her wrist comm and flung it away.

The ground became more uneven, and she stumbled and fell, got up and staggered off, wiping the tears with her grimy hands. The temperature was dropping quickly and, for the first time, she noticed the dwindling light. She stopped and looked around, having no idea where she was. The desolate landscape looked equally uninviting in all directions. She was despondent and mentally numb, but her primordial instinct of self-preservation was beginning to surface. She looked away from the dying light and saw an obstruction in the distant flat landscape. She ran toward it as the light dimmed, and the cold intensified.

Her hands were going numb, and her face was stinging with cold, and she ran. She knew she was losing her energy, and the cold was becoming brutal. Her pace was slowing, but she could make out a shape ahead which was not part of a natural horizon.

She moved toward it until she recognized one of the survival pods Krey had told her about. She tried to hurry, but her muscles were retaliating and refusing to respond normally. She felt as if she were in a terrible dream where she was moving in slow motion, until she finally reached this small structure built low into the ground. She stumbled around one side, past the plants whose leaves had curled into hard kernels against the cold. She kept moving her hands along the walls, groping until she found the opening with two steps leading down to the door. She almost fell inside when the door opened and a light came on. She collapsed onto a cushioned bench and hugged her body trying to get warm, and thankfully, could already feel heat radiating from the floor. The pod walls were solid except for a high window next to the door and one on the back wall. The air felt old and stale, but she could feel fresher air starting to circulate. She shivered and rocked back and forth and felt confused and lost in the universe.

49

Krey's body, worn from travel, ran fueled on adrenaline, driven by worry, with his eyes constantly scanning in front of him, looking for a figure in the distance. He saw the waning daylight with the impending danger and ignored it. He should have called a drone, but his mind had been too scattered to think clearly. It was useless to try and track footsteps in this eerie twilight, so he ran away from the house without a logical plan. He couldn't lose Mara. He had already lost a person he loved; it would be unbearably painful to lose another.

The thought crazed him, causing him to run and ignore the near vanishing light and the precipitous drop in temperature. He slowed when he thought his lungs were ready to burst. He took gasping breaths, trying to breathe the icy air through his nose as he squinted into the darkened horizon. His hands were shaking too much now to get any information from his wrist comm. He knew he needed to return to shelter, but the thought of Mara being out here frightened him more than the deadly cold.

He was near the point of total despair when his eyes detected a faint mirage of light ahead. He jogged toward it until his mind recognized the survival pod. *Be there, Mara, be there*. It had to be her; there was no other reason for a light. His body was spent; if she wasn't there, he couldn't go on without risking hypothermia and death.

He stumbled up to the structure, grasped the handle with numb fingers, heaved too much weight against the door, and burst inside, startling Mara. He shoved the door closed and leaned against the wall for support, his entire body flooding with relief when he saw her.

She was crumpled in the corner of the bench leaning against the wall, her arms around her knees curled up against her chest. He watched her while sucking in great breaths of air, finally able to say only, "Mara," and sat down next to her, rubbing his achingly cold hands.

She was a pitiful sight with a tear-stained face and bedraggled hair.

"This is not my home. Why am I here?" Her voice was angry and shrill, but when she looked at him her eyes filled again. "I need to go back home and find out who I am."

He winced at the words, which felt like his heart had been stung. He wanted to slap them away, out into the cold, vicious air, where each word could break into a million brittle pieces and die and never be heard again. He wanted to shout and ask her if she was crazy, thinking she could go home, as if it were around the corner. Before he could say anything, his wrist comm signaled a call from Bertie.

"Krey, we're showing a light at survival pod six. Is that you? Is Mara with you? Do we need to send out drones or Rescue?"

He answered, trying to collect any vestige of calmness. "It's me, and I have Mara here. We'll be fine until morning. Please inform Rescue that we don't need help."

"Thank God, we've been worried sick. Is Mara all right?"

Krey looked at Mara's sad and troubled figure and said, "Thanks, Bertie. She's fine, we'll see you in the morning."

What else could he say? Now he just wanted some uninterrupted time to talk with her. She was looking at him with narrow eyes. "Who am I? I don't even know who I am."

He tried to put him arm around her, but she put her feet down on the floor and leaned back, trying to retreat further into the corner.

"Who am I? I need to know who I am. Why am I here?" She was shivering, looking like a lost and wretched soul.

He opened a drawer beneath the bench and pulled out a blanket and a container of water. He unfolded the blanket and placed it over her legs. She immediately pulled it up to her shoulders.

"Would you like some water?" he asked. She shook her head to decline. He sat back down and took a long drink, wishing he had something much stronger.

"Why am I here?" she started. "What happened to me?"

He didn't know where to start. She looked like he felt, frightened and upset because neither knew the best answers.

He leaned back, resting his head against the wall and closing his eyes, wishing he could reset this whole mess.

Trying desperately to sort out where to start and what he needed to say and searching for the best words, he at last sat up, took a deep breath, and began with a bluntness brought from fatigue.

"You're here because you signed up; you requested to come."

50

Mara looked thunderstruck. Her dark eyes were boring into him. "I don't think so. Why would I do that? Surely I would remember that."

He shook his head with the first hint of disbelief and impatience. "Mara, listen to yourself. Of course, you don't remember. You haven't regained that memory yet."

Unsatisfied, she countered, "Why would I volunteer to come here?"

"I have no idea what your mind is ready to hear. But I can tell you that you signed up because you, like the rest of us here, saw that the social structure on Earth was deteriorating. It all started long before we were born and gradually progressed, sliding downward. Looking back, it's hard to understand how it got so bad without people realizing what was going on. They say it started out so gradually that no one thought the changes would affect them. It was like everyone slowly became brainwashed. Things that were good and decent gradually became reviled, and bad behaviors were accepted or promoted as long as it helped a few into power and control. Aided by the increased use of artificial intelligence, the powerful began controlling information and the language, repeating what they wanted everyone to believe. Eventually people heard the lies so often, they couldn't remember what was true.

They dismissed the individual histories of nations and promoted their new alliance, Oneworld."

"How did I get here?" she demanded, trying, without success, to remember and process what she was hearing.

"I'm getting to that," Krey went on. "The communities here on Cytar have been here for quite a while. They were originally established as exploratory expeditions, hoping to find new minerals and ores. The extents of the success on Cytar, and even many of the Earth space programs, were kept largely secret from the general population, hoping the missions could bring more wealth and power to the few. Those who didn't rely on state news sought their own information from primary sources, and they began to realize that facts and information were being withheld or distorted. They feared that suffering would increase and total chaos and destruction could occur.

"The more concerned citizens began to network with others who shared the same apprehensions and began enlisting thoughtful, skilled people, anyone who had not altered their minds with drugs and were still able to process information and think critically. They sought out people who would be willing to travel to Cytar and attempt to build a rational population, maintain a decent society in peace and, hopefully, preserve the human race."

She was watching him intently now, not interrupting. He could not read her expression so he continued, hoping it would help her understand.

"The long-journey travelers were shocked both times they returned to the Mars and moon base stations and heard and saw what was happening at home. They were stunned when they heard of the rapidity of the growth of artificial intelligence on Earth. When the shuttles were sent in, and the procurement team saw the extent of the dysfunction, they began withholding information on the advancements of our development here. They began sending misinformation that life was not sustainable here over any period of time, and that our settlement was rapidly failing. Meanwhile, the use of AI on Earth only continued to increase. That's when our travelers began in earnest to network with those trying to save a free way of life."

He stopped here, wondering if he should go on. He was tired and beyond being able to filter the narrative. If she wanted to know where she came from and how things were, he would tell her.

"The most dangerous and ironic thing about all this, the sad irony of all ironies, is that all the technology Oneworld developed to implement their plans and track their citizens ultimately became their chimera. The AI systems eventually developed to the point it didn't need humans anymore."

She was silently staring at him. He paused, searching for the words to elucidate this unfathomable information.

"The programs which artificial intelligence developed without humans were so complex, that the original developers of the early systems no longer could completely comprehend how the programs worked, or how they were able to develop such complex independent learning. The AI knew how to write its own code, self-assemble many structures, build whatever it needed, and people basically got in the way, other than to assist them in basic tasks. The roles became reversed."

He didn't wait for a response, but quickly continued. "AI monitored everyone's interests, knew what the public was watching, where they went, the people they associated with, their feelings about events. With that knowledge, they manipulated the information people received so that it aligned with the programs' goals, to keep people divided in an effective effort to enhance its own goals. People became irrelevant. Once that happened, AI implemented its own software to begin trimming the population, starting in the largest cities."

An expression of shock flooded Mara's face. It reflected a face which had absorbed too much tragic news and sadness. It was the expression of someone who had just discovered the terrible realization that she was completely powerless to change too many wrongs.

"You're telling me a nightmare." Her voice, barely audible, now sounded powerless, defeated. "I can't even comprehend how awful all that would be. How would they do that?"

"It was easy for AI to accomplish, really. They controlled the food production and distribution programs. Everyone's medical records were handled through their technology. They started changing or withholding medications or altering procedures. Many populations were decreasing on their own. Through the decades, the structure of the family had broken down, some say purposefully, and many people no longer wanted children. Many in the large metropolitan areas were becoming effectively infertile, and doctors claimed there were no known causes. And there was at least one instance I know of where AI used violence against the population, when some groups decided to resist and tried to rewrite programs. The humans were a hapless match against the speed and agility of AI data retrieval, output and implementation, and its structure only grew stronger."

"That's why everyone here is so careful with the Helper programing."

"Exactly. We've seen the consequences of uninhibited AI expansion, and we're trying to be proactive. Everyone knew what artificial intelligence could do, but few truly understood how it actually worked. Those who did comprehend the dangers, tried to warn about the eventual outcomes, but all their concerns fell on deaf ears."

He was looking at the sad figure before him, with her feet back up on the bench, watching him with her head resting on her knees.

"I know this is probably way too much information at once. Do you want me to stop?"

"No, I need to hear," she insisted.

"In our Cytar history, we've taken three arduous trips back that I know of, one early on, and two in more recent times, of which I was a part, so I speak from firsthand experience. They were long and very dangerous, unpredictable voyages. On this last trip, we communicated only with members of their workforce we knew to be understanding and sympathetic with our concerns for society and the human race. We actually used veiled communication signals off the main grid to get a shuttle into the Mars station, and from there our team traveled covertly on Oneworld ships to Earth. We stayed undercover whenever we were there, ostensibly working for the world government, but we also made arrangements to pick up extra supplies, and believe me, supplies to the general population were getting harder and harder to obtain there. It became increasingly more dangerous, but we kept enlisting any Candidates who shared our beliefs and were physically able to make the long journey."

"And I signed up?"

"Yes, from what I've been told, all of the Candidates who traveled with us understood the dangers on Earth and were helping in some way, either delivering messages, gathering scientific work, securing the dwindling supplies, suggesting Candidates or volunteering themselves when they saw how difficult the situation was becoming. I don't know anything else. I'm not sure what your role was, but I know that everyone is here because they volunteered to come."

He knew of the volunteers' hunger for survival, for preserving the history of free nations with their glories and downfalls. He had tasted the frustrations of living in a controlled, spiraling society, which had prompted his own choice to leave.   He had also read her files, but he was so tired, and he knew Tanak would be the better person to go into any details of her background. She was still questioning.

"Why didn't the other people who were helping just come themselves instead of recruiting other people?"

"Many of them were in unfavorable positions because of family members or age or health. They weren't able to take on the difficult expedition, but they wanted a better future for others and were willing to sacrifice and work for what they hoped would be the survival of the human race."

Mara leaned her head against the wall. A tear rolled down her sallow cheek. "This is a lot of horrible stuff to take in."

He heard pain and defeat in her voice. "I know. I know. Here, please drink some water."

She took a sip and handed it back to him.

"What happened to my memory?"

"We don't have the supplies, water or air filtration systems to have more than about 30 or 35 people active for the entire duration of the travel. Remember, in deep space we can never be sure of the exact length of a voyage. All of the Candidates are put in a coma-like, inactive state to conserve food and air. Tanak and his team oversee the medications for this, which include a memory block to keep the mind calm during the extended sedation. When it's time to wake up, the sedative medication is reduced, while Tanak's special wake-up cocktail is gradually increased. A few people never retrieve past memories, just happily build new ones; but most of them eventually begin to slowly remember as new information and life experiences on Cytar stimulate them. You must be an exception; you woke up so early before the wake-up protocols had even started, and now you're having these severe memory flashes."

"Hmm, lucky me," she said sarcastically.

"Mara, please try to understand. I love you. I'm so happy with our life, and you were doing so well here."

"I can't keep having these memory bursts," she said miserably. "They make me think I'm going crazy. They either need to stop, or I need to remember everything."

He took her hand then and held it with both hands, and they sat looking every bit like the exhausted couple they were.

"I'm going to be here for you, for us, until we figure this out. We'll see if Tanak can tell us what's happening and how to help. If anybody can get answers for us, he can. It's going to be okay." *It has to be okay.*

51

They were quiet after that. Krey leaned his head against the wall and closed his eyes. Mara, too tired to sort out all she'd heard, studied his haggard face. He must be beyond tired, just returning from a difficult trip, yet he still fought the perilous cold and found her. Through the confusion, her feelings for him persisted, winding their way through her jumbled mind until they formed into rational thought. She saw the solid man he was, one she could depend on, one who wouldn't flinch or give up in the rough times. He would stay with her as long as she needed him. He had come for her despite his exhaustion because he loved her, she knew that much.

They drifted in and out of sleep, with the frigid night winds whistling over the little shelter, until Krey woke and saw the morning light begin to seep through the windows. While Mara slept, he communicated with Bertie, letting him know what had happened with the memory flashes, trying to forestall too many questions. After the miserable night, the Gsport was summoned, and they returned home where a worried Gracelyn and Bertie were waiting. Neither of them mentioned the disheveled and worn-out appearances before them.

"Glad you're both okay; you had us worried," Bertie said. "I bet a hot shower sounds good to you."

"Sure does, and some fresh clothes," Krey said as they hurried in.

When they came back out after getting cleaned up, although weary but more like themselves, Gracelyn had hot coffee and breakfast ready for them. It was the last of her precious coffee reserve, but if ever there was a need for it, she thought it was now.

She didn't ask anything, but hugged Mara and said, "Everything will be all right. We'll get through this together."

Mara had a severe headache, but having her little support team gave her comfort. When they had finished eating, she went to their bedroom and slept most of the morning. While she rested, Krey had some serious mental confrontations with himself. He was upset that she even thought about going back to see her home, an almost impossible undertaking. He desperately wanted her to continue with their life here, and he wanted her to be happy living with him. He went to his office and had a long video call with Tanak to fill him in on the serious problems they were having. Krey urgently needed to find out about options and to ask for help from his friend.

Tanak was shocked at the tension and hardness showing in Krey's face. "I'm going to leave here right away. I'll meet you at my Gateway office in three hours. In the meantime, get some rest. I understand how distressing this is, but I have faith in Mara. She'll come through this fine," he said, hoping he could believe his own confident voice.

Krey was able to get a brief rest before he and Mara met Tanak in a small room in the medical office in the Gateway complex. The three sat in a tight semicircle of chairs near a wall lined with streamlined shelves and cabinets. Tanak asked Mara to describe her memory flashes, and he listened with compassion, never interrupting, until she was finished talking.

"Perhaps Krey has explained to you why we heavily sedate our Candidates. What you may not realize is the need for the memory block we administer. Without that medication, the mind can play terrible tricks when left idle for that length of time. You could awaken with neurosis, paranoia, or any manner of psychosis, which sadly can happen to long term coma patients. We have had great success with this procedure, with the exception of your early wake-up, for which quite frankly, I have found no explanation. Luckily, your mind is sharp and you show no signs of mental problems, but I understand how these unpredictable memory flares are very disturbing."

His directness and calmness were a comfort to both Mara and Krey. Here was someone who understood their crisis, and had the knowledge and the ability to help them.

"I understand that you want these unexpected flare-ups to stop, and that you've mentioned you want to return home to learn more about yourself. I'm sure you spoke in a moment of frustration. You must realize how difficult, if not impossible, that would be." The last statement was said with such finality that Mara knew the subject of travel to home would never be considered as a possible solution to her problem.

"Would you be interested in trying some induced memory therapy which may bring back much of the information you're seeking?"

She did not hesitate, "Yes, I think I need to try something. I can't have these erratic, intense recurrences. They're too painful, and they're beginning to haunt me."

"You need to recognize that once we start this process, we can't stop it until your past and present experiences logically align in your thoughts. I'll be monitoring your brain scans throughout the entire procedure. Do you both understand what I'm saying?" Now, he looked intensely at Mara. "Once we start this, I can't withdraw the medication I'm going to give you until I see your brain waves behave normally."

"I understand, and I need to do this."

Tanak turned inquiringly to Krey, who was nervous about the possibility of a negative outcome of regained memory. What if she absolutely decided she did not want to be with him, or not even want to live in Gateway at all?

Worry lines were forming between his eyebrows. He released a deep pent-up breath before he answered.

"I understand what you're saying, but I don't think this is my decision to make. I want what's best for Mara. Is this safe, and how long will all this take?"

"There are no guarantees with any medical treatment, but I wouldn't suggest this if I thought it was too dangerous for her. Because she is already having so many early memories, I don't think this will take very long. If you'd like, we can start tomorrow morning."

Mara looked at Krey, and he tried not to show his feelings, wanting this to be her decision.

"Yes, I'd like to start tomorrow," she confirmed. "I need to start tomorrow."

Tanak tried to give them both reassuring smiles.

"All right. I'll spend the night in Gateway tonight so we can start here, first thing in the morning."

At home that evening, they had serious discussions when Krey expressed his deep concerns about how this procedure could affect her and their life together. He told her that he was worried that the process might not work, or possibly have a detrimental effect on her, maybe making her unhappy or more unsettled. He loved her and needed her here with him. She understood his concerns, but was adamant. She needed to remember her past, hopefully to stop the uncontrollable memory spikes, and for their successful and happy future together.

52

They arrived early the next morning, back in the same office, wearing determined expressions and holding hands for support. Mara was seated in a reclining chair facing an artificial window light box. Tanak lowered her chair until her body was in a resting position, her short boots supported on the elevated leg rest. The window light changed into a tranquil scene of a wispy fog floating over trees and through a mystical golden light.

Krey was asked to take the seat behind her, near the door, in case he wanted to leave. The comment was not reassuring as he sat clenching and unclenching his nervous hands, with one leg resting on his knee, and the free foot shaking back and forth, unable to be still. His mind alternated between moments of calmness because of his confidence in Tanak and dizzying waves of uneasy apprehension about the procedure.

"I'll be right here; I'm not leaving her," he answered decisively.

"Let's begin then," Tanak said as he placed a thin band across Mara's forehead and one around her ankle. The lights were dimmed. "I'm going to start the medicine now. Your job is to relax; you're going to feel sleepy now. Just allow your memories to flow. Are you ready?"

She nodded and closed her eyes as he placed a bracelet holding a rectangular medication pack against the inside of her wrist. She kept her eyes closed, thinking that nothing was happening, and waited.

The first images are so bright. Warm sunshine on tanned skin, a gently rocking, streamlined personal water transport with fishing lines in the water. Peaceful, quiet, sleepy. She can smell the water and the fabric of the transport cushions and hear the water lightly lapping on the side of the craft. Her father and mother are there with her, each sitting near a fishing line which makes little weak ripples when rocked in the calm water. Her mother is wearing a sunhat and looking across the lake, watching the light bouncing off the tips of the gentle waves. It is so pleasant here, she wants to stay, but the dreams begin melting and changing, flowing in and out before she can pause them.

A new scene, blurry at first, and now sharply focused shows mesmerizing, rolling waves spiraling out behind a water cruiser. The craft moves effortlessly and swiftly over a lake smooth as glass on a beautiful summer day. Her friend Rene is with her, and they are laughing. They are traveling on an impulse to Strawberry Island to swim. When they arrive, the coordinates are set to keep the craft stationary before they jump in the shallow water. Just as she can feel the cool, smooth sand between her toes, this image melts into a different time and place.

Her father and mother are back, accompanying her into the country for a picnic. They are holding hands, hiking on a path through lush green grass, up a brilliantly sunlit hill toward tall deciduous and evergreen trees. But when she tries to follow them, they begin to fade, and her mind tells her they are gone now, never to return.

Her brother is here, looking like a movie star, driving a silver-gray convertible, one hand on the manual control, one resting on the personal transport door, showing off muscled biceps.

Now her sister is here, laughing, looking beautiful and turning heads in that new dress, and then, in some imperceptible way, she knows they are both gone. She tries to call out to them, but they fade away as new images struggle through turbulent cloudy curtains trying to ensnare her.

Everything begins shifting, and she wants to return to her childhood, but it refuses to reappear. She sees herself working on a digital system and hears news on the screens around her. People are speaking with negative and accusing tones, and her mind becomes agitated. Now she hears promises. We will be cared for, do not worry, but she only becomes more nervous. The bright images are giving way to somber moods. Her friends are there with her, talking, planning, but no matter how she strains, this vision has no sensible sounds. Now the crowds are thick, and she is having trouble getting through them. She is nervous, needing to get somewhere on time. She feels agitated and disturbed.

She is on a high-speed transport. Searching in an unknown land. Explosions in a foreign territory… Deafening confusion, smoky and coughing…Anxiety and tension… Searching for the small groups of people she needs to meet…. she meets them one by one or in small groups, there are the steady workers able to reason and sort information, the scientists, doctors, engineers, technology specialists, historians, did it never end? … More discussions, more planning. She relays the information packets to them, not knowing their exact contents, but knowing it is important. So many transport travels.

And now sunshine… deep breaths in gorgeous sunshine…beautiful sailing in a fresh wind. The sail craft leans in the breeze, dipping, with the water on the starboard side rising up near her. It feels wonderful to be away. She turns toward the stern and sees Jack at the helm. He is a good man, looking forward across the water, adjusting the sails for the trimmest slice through the waves. Her bracelet with the single star, a gift from Jack, reflects the bright sunshine, creating laser-like points of light bouncing off the sails. She wants to keep sailing forever, but the water ahead turns into a foggy blankness, and when she looks back, her vision of Jack melts away.

She is in a store with a supply list. The few items scattered on the shelves look like forlorn rejects from a close-out sale. She keeps moving to different stores, making furtive connections with the network of supporters. Everything is so expensive; she keeps looking but can never find everything she needs… always searching.

Then, Jack is here in his faded, frayed ball cap. Steady Jack makes things better. She is smiling now that he is here with his positive outlook. She watches him give her an envelope. No more wrist comms, he says. Too dangerous. She goes through less crowds now, weaving around near deserted streets, trying to be inconspicuous, always moving, until she sees her destination, a seemingly never-ending huge concrete building…a warehouse, so long and bleakly gray and disturbing. She is startled, unnerved by an erupting burst of flapping wings. Pigeons. Someone is alerted by the outburst and begins walking in shadows, walking to meet until she delivers the envelope to someone in dark clothing who moves on without stopping.

Transport

The images are coming too rapidly now and become so truncated it becomes difficult to make sense of any of them. She is always in a hurry to deliver messages in person or copying files on her scanner, sending files, nervous. The algorithms in the news feeds have been changed, and they are altering the truth and sending misinformation. Working feverishly to stop it. How to make the people aware? Why can't they understand?

Someone is following her. She puts her hand in her coat pocket. The old portable data peg is there, but she needs to move faster. Why is it so cold? Keep moving. Hurry. Genna is there, Genna! She makes the handoff and blends into a small group of people. She is being followed. Hurry, move. Someone shoves her from behind. A man grabs her arm, and she is in a timeworn boxy transport before she can react. Too dark to see.

Loud grating sounds, freezing cold. The ancient sounding motor is too loud to hear any conversations clearly. Images are coming too swiftly now. She sees town lights disappear in the gray snow. The old local midair transport is flying too low into darkness. Escape or death. There are no doors; they are not watching, she pitches outward, falling, snowy mounds rushing toward her. Darkness.

A large dog is in her face, now nudging her shoulder before a man in a parka reaches her. She hobbles with him through snow to a low roofed, barely visible cabin almost buried by snow drifts against its walls. She is lying in front of a huge fire, feeling its heat on her side. Instinctively, she touches her wrist, searching for her star bracelet, needing the connection with Jack. Missing. Lost…

The sound of crackling logs captures her scattered attention, an ember, so crystal clear, escapes and dies in the air. The dog is sitting close, looking down at her. She is staring up at large round wooden beams crossing a planked wooden ceiling. She can smell the hot soup the man brings. Talking. Rapid message bursts are being sent.

It is morning. Her rescuer says it is not safe here; she needs to move. She is traveling with him on a high speed snowglider. The wind and cold are stinging her face.

Jack is waiting with a wistful smile. She can sense a bittersweet melancholy hanging heavily over him. It is time to go; others are waiting to leave, but Jack? Jack? She can feel Jack's strong arms around her, but he is not coming with her? He needs to stay and help here; she is clutching the arm of his jacket. Her heart is pounding. Hurry. Go. Stick with the plan. Get everyone on board before it's too late. You'll be needed there.

She sees Tanak. Tanak is waiting… She is quiet, peaceful…

"Mara, Mara," she could hear Tanak's calm, patient voice coming across a distant abyss. "Mara, you can wake up now."

When she opened her eyes, he was standing near her, the medication pack was gone, and he was removing the bands, while Krey held her hand. She could not yet respond; the images were still so vivid and disturbing.

"Can you hear me?" It was Krey, looking distraught.

"Yes," she whispered with a far-off look. She was slowly beginning to realize where she was.

"I saw so many places."

Tanak brought her water. She took a cautious sip, and sat back, exhausted and closed her eyes. "How long was I out?"

"You've been dreaming off and on for almost three hours. You should rest for a while," Tanak advised, but she was already drifting off.

"Krey, we need to let her rest now while the medication has a chance to dissipate, and you, my friend, look like an abandoned stray."

Tanak began leading him to a café. Krey remembered bringing Mara here the first time he took her to his work, when she first started realizing where she was.

"You need to eat something. Mara is going to be fine," Tanak said encouragingly.

"Is she going to remember me and our life here?"

"None of her present memories should have changed. Her brain scan looked perfectly normal, better than when we started. The memory block on the *Superstes* was strictly to keep the mind calm during the extended coma. I kept the medications for this recall quite benign because she was already remembering so much. We'll know more after she rests. Her mind has just been through an exhausting effort. It may take a while to process it all and see if she can fill in the pieces when she's fully awake. She'll have a lot to think about, and we'll need to be here to support her and give her time to sort her new memories out."

53

Gracelyn could not wait another minute. After thinking too much about how Mara and Krey were doing, she left work early and stopped at the medical office to see them. She found Mara sitting up, drinking tea and looking tired but serene and thoughtful and happy to see her friend.

"Mara, how are you feeling? Where is Krey?" She sat next to her, leaning forward as if to hear better.

"Krey is with Tanak, I think. He looked so worried and worn out when I woke up. I saw so much, Gracelyn. I remember my family."

She wore a somewhat melancholy smile, but then looked more serious. "Were things that bad when you were back on Earth?"

Gracelyn reflected for a moment, closing her eyes and shaking her head, and then, as if an overfilled bottle tipped, the words began pouring out.

"Things were getting sad to see before Bertie and I left. I think the means to help people were there at one time, but the countries that were capable of good change fell into the hands of a cadre of individuals who, for whatever reason, banded together and used all the resources for their own personal power and gain. They incorporated more and more AI systems to expedite strategies, effectively cutting the citizens out of the loop. Oh, I think some of them initially thought they were doing what was right, but when they realized the true motives, things had already reached a tipping point, and they couldn't stop the damage.

"Once this group controlled most of the information outlets and disseminated their propaganda, it was hard to wrest back any control. The young were particularly vulnerable to the lies because they had less life experiences, had less knowledge of history, and were more easily influenced. Those in control seemed to know exactly how to influence them. And when they swayed and bribed government officials to legalize all of the new classes of drugs, enticing them with the profits to be made, it looked pretty hopeless. People failed or didn't care to recognize the detrimental consequences to the entire social structure until the downward spiral began. Or, who knows, maybe they wanted a drugged-up population because they're more easily manipulated."

She paused and sighed. "I should stop. I've already said more than you need to hear now."

Mara was looking intently at Gracelyn, trying to take in these new revelations, mixed in with her medically induced recalls and all of Krey's disclosures from the survival pod. It was an immense amount of new information to take in, but the most intense discoveries were her newly recovered memories.

"I remember now that I was trying to help, and it was very difficult. Were you helping, too? Is that how you decided to come here?"

"Yes, Bertie and I both tried to help, but we left before you did, and I know things got worse. We were already working in the space program in ground support, so it was an easy decision for us when the opportunity came up."

"I didn't realize. I thought I needed to go back and find myself. I'm still processing everything, but the images that were recalled today were not what I imagined. I think I'm feeling more reconciled with my place here now, and why I'm here. I know I was leaving to come here, even chose to come here. But I don't know if I'm more dreadfully sad or overwhelmingly angry when I think about how life became so mixed up in such a beautiful place. I realize what I miss here. I miss the water and ocean waves and the abundant plant life and all the birds and wildlife. Don't you miss that?"

"Yes, I miss it; we all do. I don't think we'll ever get over that, because we've seen its beauty. But we can't look back because there's no use in it. We have to be grateful that we found a place to survive, and be thankful to all those who sacrificed to make this possible. And I'm always amazed when I think of the incredible progress that has been made here."

She smiled kindly at Mara before continuing. "I'm so happy to hear that you've regained some memories and can be content here. You must know now that going back was probably not ever an option, and even if it were, that journey is just so unpredictable and dangerous, I doubt we'll ever go back. For all practical purposes, this was a one-way trip. Besides, you're needed here, Mara. Krey needs and loves you. This is your home now, where you are loved." She placed her hand over Mara's for emphasis.

Just then the door opened and Tanak walked in followed by an anxious looking Krey. Tanak smiled, "Wow, the women are already talking. That's a good sign."

Gracelyn got up to leave, "Just getting caught up on some things. I'll see you back at the house, Mara." She gave a supportive squeeze to Krey's arm before she left the room.

"How are you feeling now?" Tanak asked as Mara stood up.

"I feel exhausted, but mentally much better. The memories began piling up. It was so strange; some of the images were so complete and vivid, and others so vague. I remembered so much, and some of the little details are just beginning to emerge and hopefully will continue to become clearer. I only saw brief snapshots of my life, so I'm hoping more will fill in."

"I now think your memory is where is should be at this point," Tanak reassured her. "As you work and learn and have new experiences here, they will trigger things from your pre-journey life, and your background will slowly begin to become clearer. You should be able to assimilate all your memories at a more reasonable rate. That's how it was supposed to happen for you, and how it's happened for most of our travelers, although, as you've heard, a very few retain pre-travel amnesia, and still adjust well to life here."

She was listening closely, contemplating this information, particularly about how her memories could improve.

"I think I'm so lucky to have you here, Tanak. Thank you so much for your help. I can't say that enough." She was looking sincerely at him before turning her pale face to Krey.

"I'm mentally exhausted; can we go home now?" Relief flooded over Krey's face, but before he could answer, Tanak spoke to Mara.

"Yes, go home, but I'll being doing several checkups for a while, just to make sure you're not having any strange memory issues. I don't think you will now, but I want to keep observing to be sure."

"I already feel better, like my body and mind are more relaxed and in the same place, if that makes any sense. I just need time to think and review all of this in my mind. I'm so grateful for all you've done, Tanak," she reiterated. She gave him a hug, and Krey gave him a powerful thank you handshake before they headed to their transport.

54

Krey's arm was around her as soon as they were in the Gsport, and he kept it there the whole way home. She rested her head on his shoulder and was quiet. When they arrived home, she went straight to the dining area and stared for some time through the clear door at the backyard, her face expressionless. She stood for a while before she turned to the cooking area, looked at the picture over the counter, and then slowly took in the table and the cabinets, as if seeing them with the new perspective of her permanent home. The fresh memory of her former home surfaced, making her realize how small and compact this structure was in comparison.

Then, she looked over at Krey and, for what seemed like a long while, studied him with an understanding of the qualities and the strength of his character, which she had come to rely upon. He had been standing there, leaning against the wide door frame for support, with his thumb tucked in his jeans' pocket, just watching her, trying to read her expression and hoping like hell she still wanted to be with him. They stood looking with eyes locked for a long moment before the corners of her mouth hinted at turning up.

"I think I'm a little hungry," she said softly at last, with one of her gentle smiles that he couldn't wait to see every day. "Do you want anything?"

His eyes closed briefly, and he nodded. "Yes, absolutely," he said, matching her smile, and grateful for the wall supporting his relief-filled body. This sounded and looked more like his Mara. Gladness began to fill his mind and flow through him. Earlier, he felt like his insides had been twisted into knots, and he hadn't wanted to think about food when he went out with Tanak; but as he relaxed, he could feel some faint indications of hunger.

They ate together as they usually did, as if it was an ordinary day, and he let her lead the conversation even though he had so many questions. She barely tasted the food, her head so filled with new images and her newly remembered experiences. He never thought a simple meal tasted so delicious, sitting there listening to the voice that he needed to hear.

At one point, they became quiet before she looked at him with a face reflecting deep concern and asked, "Are we going to be okay?"

He reached over and rested his hand over her wrist. He sat for several moments, just staring at their hands, before he looked up and spoke in a reassuring, matter-of-fact tone.

"Yeah, we're going to be okay. We'll have to keep working hard in this crazy place, and it won't be easy; sometimes it will be terribly difficult, but we'll get through it. We'll have some good times and some tough times, but we're going to be okay. I'll try to be strong for you when you need me to, and you'll try and be strong for me when I need you to, and we'll be okay."

Transport

She studied his face again and thought about all the unknowns in their future before nodding an understanding.

Afterwards, they went to the sitting room and just sat quietly together while she slowly began to tell him about her family and some of the memory fragments she experienced. The medications and mind journey were taking their toll, and she soon felt drained and needed to rest. They stood up, but before she left the room, she looked deeply at him with moist eyes, leaned in and kissed him. It was a long kiss that said, "I love you; I'll always love you, and I'm going to be with you." He held her for some time in an almost crushing embrace before letting her go.

Later, he went into his office, opened the small cabinet by the chair, and took out a treasured bottle of fine bourbon. He had brought it with him on his first expedition back to Earth over five years ago. It was now over half empty and irreplaceable. He carefully poured himself a rare drink before sinking into his favorite chair.

He took a deep breath followed by a long sigh, and drank slowly, letting the oak-aged liquid slide down his throat as if to wash away his former worries. Mara was with him. He marveled at their journey together, two people who were brought together in desperate times through the incomprehensible vastness of the universe.
How many times had that story played out over the eons of time? He thanked whatever Being brought them together.

He didn't know their future, but he knew that they could trust in the wisdom of that Divinity which was sending them on this enigmatic journey. Immense sensations which he could not immediately identify washed over him, and then slowly, gladness and contentment filled him as he recognized those feelings.

They were the wondrous feelings of peace and hope and especially love.

Peace in the knowledge that he and Mara would continue to be together to face this new world with all of its challenges and rewards. It was a peace that travels deep into the soul and stays buried, able to repel the constant daily onslaughts that pick at the world.

The hope was for the future. A hope for the continuation of the human species living and growing here. A hope that, despite the trials, they would prevail in their own small way, just as they all were meant to.

And love. Love for Mara, for his friends and for his life. A profound love for the life that does not need to be heralded or recognized outwardly, but one that will be lived and endured in simple decency and dignity.

Peace, hope and love. He sat, while the intense awareness of the emotions cloaked him with well-being, and he knew, for that moment, everything was as it should be.

Made in the USA
Las Vegas, NV
02 December 2021

35875276R10177